APOCALYPSE NOW

Carpenter gave the world a last scrutiny. The end of days had come. He supposed he should feel pleased his dire predictions had proven true but it was hard to get excited over what might prove to be the death knell of an entire planet. "How could we do this to ourselves?"

The dark clouds and the purple flashes now filled half the sky and were sweeping toward the compound like a swarm of ethereal demons.

Slayne was hastening a few stragglers toward the bunkers.

"A penny for your thoughts?"

"You can have them for free, Diana." Carpenter nodded at the atmospheric upheaval. "The human race has rolled the dice on its existence, and the dice have come up snake eyes."

The Wilderness series writing as David Thompson:

#1: KING OF THE MOUNTAIN
#2: LURE OF THE WILD
#3: SAVAGE RENDEZVOUS
#4: BLOOD FURY
#5: TOMAHAWK REVENGE
#6: BLACK POWDER JUSTICE
#7: VENGEANCE TRAIL
#8: DEATH HUNT
#9: MOUNTAIN DEVIL
HAWKEN FURY (Giant Edition)
#10: BLACKFOOT MASSACRE
#11: NORTHWEST PASSAGE
#12: APACHE BLOOD
#13: MOUNTAIN MANHUNT
#14: TENDERFOOT
#15: WINTERKILL
#16: BLOOD TRUCE
#17: TRAPPER'S BLOOD
#18: MOUNTAIN CAT
#19: IRON WARRIOR
#20: WOLF PACK
#21: BLACK POWDER
#22: TRAIL'S END
#23: THE LOST VALLEY
#24: MOUNTAIN MADNESS
#25: FRONTIER MAYHEM
#26: BLOOD FEUD
#27: GOLD RAGE
#28: THE QUEST
#29: MOUNTAIN NIGHTMARE
#30: SAVAGES
#31: BLOOD KIN
#32: THE WESTWARD TIDE
#33: FANG AND CLAW
#34: TRACKDOWN
#35: FRONTIER FURY
#36: THE TEMPEST
#37: PERILS OF THE WIND
#38: MOUNTAIN MAN
#39: FIREWATER
#40: SCAR
#41: BY DUTY BOUND
#42: FLAMES OF JUSTICE
#43: VENGEANCE
#44: SHADOW REALMS
#45: IN CRUEL CLUTCHES
#46: UNTAMED COUNTRY
#47: REAP THE WHIRLWIND
#48: LORD GRIZZLY
#49: WOLVERINE
#50: PEOPLE OF THE FOREST (Giant Edition)
#51: COMANCHE MOON
#52: GLACIER TERROR
#53: THE RISING STORM
#54: PURE OF HEART
#55: INTO THE UNKNOWN
#56: IN DARKEST DEPTHS
#57: FEAR WEAVER
#58: CRY FREEDOM
#59: ONLY THE STRONG

ENDWORLD: DOOMSDAY

DAVID ROBBINS

LEISURE BOOKS  NEW YORK CITY

Dedicated to Judy, Joshua and Shane.

A LEISURE BOOK®

April 2009

Published by

Dorchester Publishing Co., Inc.
200 Madison Avenue
New York, NY 10016

ISBN 10: 0-8439-6232-1
ISBN 13: 978-0-8439-6232-1
E-ISBN: 1-4285-0652-7

Printed in the United States of America.

10 9 8 7 6 5 4 3 2 1

ENDWORLD: DOOMSDAY

"Some say there are four ages of man. Some say there are five. Others say the total is twelve. But there is no set number. Human history is not a straight line. It is a circle. A circle of cycles. Humans rise and they fall. They create and they destroy, and then create from that which fell to begin a new cycle all over again. That is the nature of things."

—*The Book of Secret Truth*

Future Tense

Minnesota

They were going to do it.

They were going to destroy the world.

Kurt Carpenter stared at the TV screen in the back of his limousine and tried to wrap his mind around what he was seeing. Mushroom clouds. Mushroom clouds in the Middle East. A third of Israel, reduced to cinders. She had retaliated with her own nuclear arsenal, of course, and now the announcer was saying that there were five confirmed nuclear explosions in the country that had attacked. Five cities, wiped out.

Carpenter leaned back and closed his eyes. He willed himself to relax but couldn't. How could anyone relax with the end of the world about to take place? He swallowed, or tried to, but his mouth was too dry. "God in heaven." He clenched his fists so hard, his fingernails dug into his palms. "We're really going to do it."

The "we" was all-inclusive, as in "the human race."

Carpenter had long believed that humankind would shoot itself in the head, but he'd also hoped, desperately hoped, that his fellow humans would prove him wrong.

"Do we turn back, sir?"

Holland was looking at him in the rearview mirror. As usual, the chauffeur could have been carved from stone for all the emotion he showed.

"Back to the airport?" Carpenter shook his head. "No. We go on to the compound. The word must go out."

"Will there be time, sir, for everyone to get there? What if the government grounds all flights?"

"We keep our fingers crossed."

Carpenter mentally crossed his own. He had planned for so long. He had worked so hard. A lot of people thought he was nuts. They sneered and snickered behind his back. A few laughed at him to his face. "What a waste of your money!" was the common sentiment.

But the way Carpenter saw it, what good was a fortune if it wasn't put to good use? And what better use than to salvage what he could so that humanity would survive to build a new world from the ruins of the old?

The news channel cut to world leaders reacting to the crisis. Every last one was deeply shocked. Every last one was determined that whoever was to blame would pay. Saber rattling George Armstrong Custer would be proud of.

It was a long drive from the Twin Cities to Lake Bronson State Park. Normally, Carpenter used the time to go over scripts and note camera angles and special lighting and lens effects. Or he might do paperwork for financing an upcoming project. Or any number of things related to his work as a movie director.

But not today. All Carpenter could think of was the apocalypse and those he could save if only they were able to reach the compound before it was too late.

Philadelphia

Soren Anderson was working on the thirtieth floor of a skyscraper under construction in the heart of the City of Brotherly Love. He handled the one-shot rivet gun with an ease few men could match. His size had a lot to do with it. Soren was a few inches shy of seven feet tall, with broad shoulders and arms bulging with muscle. Add to that his shoulder-length blond hair and his blond mustache and neatly trimmed beard, and it was no wonder most who saw him thought he was Scandinavian or Danish.

Soren was Norwegian. Or his great-great-great-great-great grandfather had been. Not that it mattered to Soren; he saw himself as American, born and bred. He knew as much about Norway, except in one respect, as he did about, say, Outer Mongolia.

Soren was bent over the rivet gun, checking the air regulator, when someone clapped him on the back. He turned and was surprised to find the foreman, Carl Nestor. "I'm going as fast as I can."

Nestor had a strange look about him and kept glancing at the sky.

"It's not that. We're calling it quits for the day. Get your stuff and get out of here."

Soren didn't hide his surprise. "But it's only two. Three hours yet until quitting time. Why so early?"

"You wouldn't have heard on account of this." Nestor tapped the rivet gun. "We all need to leave."

Soren noticed that nearly every other member of the crew was gone and the few still left were making for the elevator. "What in Odin's name is going on?"

"Hurry," Nestor urged. "You have a long ride to reach your family before it hits the fan."

"Before what does?"

Carl Nestor didn't answer. Instead, he did a strange thing. He held out his hand, and when Soren shook it, Nestor said, "In case this is the real deal, it's been a pleasure knowing you, you big lug. You're one of the good guys."

"What are you talking about?"

Bewildered, Soren watched the foreman join those leaving. He set the rivet gun down, took off his work gloves, and pushed his hard hat back on his tousled mane of blond hair. Only then did he hear the sirens. His bewilderment growing, he moved to the edge of the girder and stared down at the city where he'd grown up. To the northeast, the Benjamin Franklin Bridge gleamed in the sunlight. If not for the smog, he'd be able to see clear to Camden.

Something was wrong. Soren had never seen so many people on the sidewalks. The streets were bumper to bumper. Horns blared in constant cacophony, punctuated by the shrill scream of scores of sirens.

"Has everyone gone mad?" Soren wondered aloud. He thought of his wife and children, the three people he loved most in the world, and alarm spiked through him.

Soren picked up his tool belt on his way to the elevator. He strapped the belt around his waist as he waited. No one else was around. He was the last to go down. He listened to the whine of the cable and the grind of gears as the lift climbed to his level. The car rattled to a stop. Anxiously, he exited, muscles tensed. He was mildly shocked when he reached the parking lot to find that his half-ton pickup was the only vehicle left. He was reaching into his front pocket for his keys when his phone chirped.

Soren answered it.

"Mr. Anderson, this is Becca Levy. This isn't a test or a drill. I repeat, this isn't a test or a drill."

"All-Father, no," Soren said. So he had been right. His worst fear was about to be made real.

"What is your password, sir?"

"Sif."

"I am instructed to tell you that the Endworld Protocol is active."

"How much time do I have?"

"One hundred hours, remember? Can you make it to the compound in that amount of time, Mr. Anderson?"

"I'll get my family there or die trying."

"I wish you luck, Mr. Anderson. You have farther to travel than most. If at any time we can be of assistance, contact the Communications Center. We'll have people manning the phones 24–7."

"Thank you." Soren closed his phone and again reached into his pocket for his keys. Nearby, someone coughed. He turned, his eyes widening slightly. He hadn't expected anything like this so soon.

There were five of them, gangstas sporting their colors, cold arrogance stamped on their young faces. The tallest bobbed his chin at the pickup. "Hey, man. That yours?"

"Yes," Soren admitted.

"We want it. Hand over the keys and everything will be cool. Give us a hard time and we'll waste you." And with that, he flicked out a knife.

Phoenix

Dr. Diana Trevor was wrapping up her last class of the day at Arizona State University.

"No one knows why this should be. Yet it's been proven again and again. The Dominant Five is not just a human phenomenon. It has been documented in animals, as well." Diana regarded the notes she had made on the blackboard. "The first practical application was by the Chinese during the Korean War. They decided to separate the more aggressive American prisoners from those who never gave them any trouble. They found that the ratio was one in twenty. One dominant for every twenty passive."

A student raised his hand. "Surely there were variables."

"The Chinese thought there would be, too. But the number was precise. It was exactly one in twenty. Or 5 percent. Subsequent research has confirmed the statistic."

Another student raised her hand. "What happened when the Chinese separated them?"

"The passives gave them no trouble whatsoever. It was the dominants who always stirred the passives up."

Yet another hand. "Is there any way to tell who is dominant and who is passive?"

"Psychological profiles have been developed, but they're not infallible, as yet." Diana allowed herself a small smile. "I should know. I developed some of them."

The buzzer brought an end to her lecture. Her students began gathering up notes and backpacks.

Diana closed her book and reached under her desk for her briefcase. She went out the side door and down the hall to the teachers' lounge. The TV in the far corner was on and nearly every instructor was glued to it. "What on earth?" Diana said.

"Shhh," someone cautioned.

A newsman was intoning gravely into the camera. Beads of sweat dotted his brow and he kept licking his lips.

> *"This just in. The president will address the nation at the top of the hour, which is twenty-seven minutes from now. Some think he will announce a declaration of war. Others, that he will impose martial law. Stay tuned to this station for live coverage."*

"What's going on?" Diana asked. No one answered.

The announcer did more lip-licking.

"To recap, war has broken out in the Middle East. The Chinese have threatened to retaliate against anyone who attacks their allies in the region. The Russians are incensed and telling the Chinese to stay out. France has called for a referendum. The United States has vowed to stand by Israel, and there is word from the Pentagon that a task force is being rushed to the region."

"It's finally happened," Diana said to herself, then backed out of the lounge. She hurried to her office. Once her door was shut, she opened her purse and took out her address book. From a plastic sleeve in the back she slid a folded piece of paper. Opening it, she dialed the number written there.

"Home Communications."

"This is Diana Trevor. My personal password is Colin. I haven't been contacted yet, but I just saw the news."

"You were right to call. We tried to reach you, Dr. Trevor. The Endworld Protocol is active."

"Dear God."

"Do you anticipate any trouble reaching the compound?"

"No," Diana said. "I have a pilot's license and my own plane."

"We advise you to hurry. If martial law is declared, all civilian flights will be grounded. If you are still in the air, the military might shoot you down."

"I'll be there as soon as I can." Diana hung up and stepped to the window. Word was spreading. A mass exodus of the campus was underway. For the most part it was orderly, but a few people were pushing and shoving.

"And so it begins." Diana shook her head in dismay at the stupidity, then turned and snatched up her briefcase. She gave her office a last look. Her framed diplomas, her keepsakes, her files—she must leave them behind. She felt no regrets. She had known this day would come and been one of the few to plan for it. Now her foresight was paying off.

The hallway was jammed. Diana stayed close to the wall until she emerged from double doors into the bright glare of the afternoon sun. The sky was clear save for a few pillowy clouds, and birds were warbling. It was hard to believe that on the other side of the world, a holocaust raged.

Vehicles jammed the parking lot exits. Tempers were short, and curses were hurled back and forth.

Diana went to her reserved parking space. She strapped her briefcase onto the back of her bike, donned her helmet, and straddled her rocket. The throb of power brought a grin. She didn't bother with the exits. She went up over the curb and zipped across a knoll to a side street and from there wound her way to 101. She headed west, looping around downtown Phoenix until she came to 303. Here the traffic was lighter. She pushed it, weaving in and out between the cars and trucks as if they were standing still. Horns blared and fingers were thrust at her. All she did was grin.

Presently Diana arrived at a small airfield west of Wittmann. It had an equally small clientele, which was why she had picked it. The major airfields, she imagined, would be disasters.

No one was in the front office. A cup of coffee had been spilled on the desk and several drawers were open.

Diana went to her locker. She took out the pack she always kept ready. Opening it, she rummaged inside, verifying its contents. Then she hastened to the side of the field where her Boena and several others were lined up in a row. She was about to climb up on the wing when someone said her name.

Harry Pierce came walking around the tail of the plane

next to hers. He held his jacket over his shoulder, and his tie was undone. Sweat stains moistened his white shirt. "Diana! Perfect timing. You're just what I need."

"How's that, Harry?"

"I'd like to hitch a ride. I've been having engine trouble. They promised to get right on it, but now it's too late."

Diana patted her aircraft. "This isn't a car, Harry. I can't drop you off anywhere you like."

"I know, I know." Harry grinned and regarded her aircraft as if admiring it. "This little hummingbird of yours is a real beaut."

"That's not what you said the last time I ran into you. As I recall, you called it a girlie plane."

"Well, you *are* a girl. And the pink stripes are a bit much." Harry patted the wing. "All fueled, are you?"

"I always keep it fueled, Harry." Diana raised her leg to climb on.

"So you won't give me a lift? Say, to Kansas City? If it's out of your way, I'll gladly pay you."

"I'm sorry, Harry. I can't. I have somewhere to be."

Overhead, an Air Force jet thundered across the heavens, streaking to the east.

"What I wouldn't give to have one of those babies," Harry said with a grin, then turned serious. "Look. No more beating around the bush. War is about to break out, and we both know what that means. I need to get to Kansas City, either with your help or without it."

"You'll have to find someone else to take you."

"Or I can fly myself," Harry Pierce said, and attacked her.

New York City

Deepak Kapur stared at the image on his computer screen and blurted the first thing that came into his head: "Shiva is unleashed." He pushed his chair back and bowed his head. "So many lives," he said softly.

His cell beeped and he answered without looking at the caller's number. "Yes?"

"Mr. Kapur, this is Becca Levy, Home Communications. Your password, please."

"Those silly passwords," Deepak said.

"If you have a complaint, sir, you may take it up with Mr. Carpenter. But right now, please, I need your password."

"I've seen the news. I know I need to get there."

"Please, Mr. Kapur."

Deepak sighed. "My password is Yama. Appropriate, don't you think?"

"Sir?"

"In my religion Yama is the lord of death. He rips souls from corpses and assigns them to what you would call hell. He will be very busy these next weeks and months and perhaps years. I hope he has some vacation time saved."

"Sir? Was that a joke?"

"Or a philosophical conundrum. Take your pick. But now that you have the password, do I win the kewpie doll?"

"Mr. Kapur, you're being morbid. Are you all right?"

"The world as we thought we knew it is coming to an end. So of course I'm all right."

"Very well, then. You're at work right now, I take it?" She rattled off the address and the floor.

"That is correct."

"Then I'm instructed to tell you to remain there. Mr. Slayne is on his way and should arrive within the next fifteen to twenty minutes."

"Who?"

"Patrick Slayne, sir. He's head of compound security. He also lives in New York, and Mr. Carpenter had dispatched him to personally see that you reach here safely.

All those considered crucial to our end-of-the-world operation are having security sent to bring them in."

"What? Preferential treatment? Why wasn't I told about this before? I'm not sure I like being treated this way."

"You're special, sir. Your computer expertise is critical. Please be ready for Mr. Slayne. He will identify himself with his password."

"Which is?"

"Mighty Mouse."

Deepak laughed, then realized she wasn't joking. "Wait. You're serious? What sort of man picks that as his password?"

"It wasn't his first choice, sir. Mr. Carpenter said his first choice was too silly and asked that he change it."

"Don't keep me in suspense, Ms. Levy."

"It was Daffy Duck."

The dial tone hummed in Deepak's ear. He shook his head and slowly set down the phone. "I've signed on with lunatics."

The image on the screen had shifted. It showed a satellite view of the eastern Mediterranean Sea. A circular cloud with a long stalk was rising to the stratosphere, glowing like the phosphorescent mushroom it resembled.

Deepak turned up the volume.

"We repeat, the carrier force dispatched to aid Israel has been obliterated. Congress is in special session and any minute now the president will address the nation. Speculation is running rampant that war will be declared."

The newscaster became even more grim.

"No one can predict whether the Chinese will carry through with their threat to attack any country that

threatens their Mideast allies. There are reports of Chinese troops massing along the Russian border. There is also a report that a fleet of North Korean submarines is bound for the West Coast of the United States, but that hasn't been confirmed."

"It's the end of all things," Deepak said softly.

"Some of us don't die so easy."

Startled, Deepak spun so fast he nearly fell out of his chair. A man stood just inside the door. He wore a dark blue trench coat over a black Rudolpho suit, white shirt and silk tie. His shoes, Kleins from Germany, were polished to a mirror finish. His hair was black, cut short with long sideburns. He had the most piercing blue eyes.

"I beg your pardon. Are you with corporate?"

"Mighty Mouse," the man said.

Deepak blinked. "Mr. Slayne? I just got off the phone with the compound. They told me you would be fifteen to twenty minutes yet."

"I ran all the red lights." Slayne stopped and seemed to be waiting. "And yours?"

"My what?"

"Mighty Mouse."

"Oh. Yama. Mine is Yama." Deepak grinned self-consciously. "Aren't those code words silly?"

"I was the one who suggested Carpenter use them."

"Really?"

Slayne offered his hand.

Bracing himself for the inevitable, Deepak shook it. He had small, delicate hands, and it upset him to no end that many men felt compelled to crush his fingers in grips of iron, as if by doing so they somehow proved how masculine they were. But to his surprise, Slayne's grip was powerful yet controlled. Only a hint of pressure and a suggestion of strength, and then the man in the blue trench coat stepped back and motioned toward the door.

"After you."

"I'm not ready yet. There are some discs I want to back up. Then we need to swing by my apartment so I can—"

Slayne held up a hand, cutting him short. "Have you looked out your window recently?"

"No. Why?"

"Maybe you should."

Deepak stood. He smoothed his Argoni jacket and went around his desk. The first thing that caught his eye, before he even reached the window, was the smoke. Columns of it, rising from several points throughout the city. He heard sirens, so many it was impossible to tell one from another. He gazed down from the vantage of the eighty-fifth floor, and even from that height, the word that leaped to his mind was "chaos." "Is it as bad as it looks?"

"Worse. There's a rumor going around that New York will be the first city nuked. Panic has set in. Every bridge, every street out is clogged. Looting has started. The police are trying their best, but there aren't enough officers to control the people in the streets. The mayor has appealed to the governor for the National Guard, but it will be tomorrow morning before the Guard can show up in any force."

"How is it you know all this? I didn't see anything about the traffic jams or the riots on the news."

"You will soon. I have other sources. In case no one has told you, I'm with Tekco. Maybe you've heard of us?"

Indeed, Deepak had. Tekco Security was global, with offices in dozens of countries. "You're in charge of protecting Carpenter's retreat? That makes sense. Tell me, what specific challenges do you foresee?"

Slayne consulted his watch. "We can talk about that later. Right now I need to get you out of New York before all hell breaks loose."

"Give me a minute." Deepak went to turn from the window when there was a loud *krump* in the distance, and the entire window shook. He was appalled to see a roiling fireball rise over the warehouse district. "Was that an explosion?"

"Yes. Hurry, please."

"What in the world is happening out there?"

"People have begun to realize this isn't a short-term crisis. Most are trying to flee before the missiles start coming our way. Those who can't flee are helping themselves to what they'll need in order to survive."

Deepak gazed down again. "Thousands of years of culture and civilization are unraveling before our eyes."

"Civilization is only skin-deep."

"I don't believe that. Deep down all people are basically good."

"Crisis tends to bring out either the best in everyone or the worst. We'll just have to see which side prevails." Slayne motioned again. "But we need to hurry."

It took a minute for Deepak to gather up his backpack and a few personal items. He followed Slayne out the door and down the long hall to the elevators. Other workers hurried out of cubicles and offices, headed in the same direction.

A portly man, sweating profusely, bustled up. "Can you believe this, Deepak? Can you fricking believe this?"

"Hey, Alf. To be honest, I've expected something like this would happen for a long time now." Deepak almost revealed more. He almost told his friend about the compound, but a sharp glance from Slayne smothered the impulse.

"You and everybody else, buddy. I thought it *might*, but I never actually thought it *would*. I mean, how crazy do you have to be to start World War Three?" Alf Richardson shook his head in disbelief.

Deepak noticed that two of the elevators were in use and the third was almost full.

"Think about it," Alf went on. "Nuclear bombs, nuclear missiles, neutron bombs, military satellites, biological weapons, chemical weapons. Does anyone seriously think the human race will survive?"

"I know one man who does," Deepak said, but his reply was lost in a sudden uproar.

A few more people were trying to squeeze into the elevator and those already in, packed shoulder to shoulder, were pushing them back out. "Take the next one," one man said each time he pushed.

"There's room for one more!" a tall man in a brown suit snapped. He had a nose like a beak and an Adam's apple as big as a golf ball. "I'm Adam Pierpoint, Vice President of Earthfind. I insist you make room for me."

Deepak knew Pierpoint fairly well and didn't like him. Earthfind was the company Deepak worked for as a programmer and systems analyst.

"There isn't any room!" the man who was doing most of the pushing insisted. "Take the next one."

The doors started to close. Adam Pierpoint stepped between them and thrust both of his spindly arms out, stopping them. "Let me in or you're not going anywhere."

"Is that so?"

The man in the elevator punched Pierpoint in the mouth. The V.P. tottered back, more shocked than hurt, although blood trickled from his bottom lip. Then the door hissed shut and pinged, and the indicator light in the wall panel showed that the elevator was descending.

Pierpoint touched a hand to his mouth and stared aghast at the blood on his finger. "Did you see what he did?" he asked no one in particular.

Another elevator was rising. It was two floors below and would be there any moment. Those waiting surged forward. One man bellowed for another to get off of his toes.

That was when Patrick Slayne faced them and held out his arms. "The next car is spoken for. All of you will have to wait a little longer."

"Says you!"

"Who do you think you are?"

Deepak was dumfounded. He realized Slayne was doing this for his benefit. "I'm not going to hog one to myself."

If Slayne heard, he didn't respond. He turned to confront Adam Pierpoint, who reared angrily over him.

Blood flecked Pierpoint's chin. He balled his bony fists and shook one at Slayne. "I've had enough of this. No one has the right to deny anyone else. You will step aside and let us enter, or else."

Deepak wondered what the "or else" meant. He tried to push past two men but they wouldn't let him by. "Excuse me, please."

"Go to hell."

Then Patrick Slayne did the last thing anyone expected. Certainly, Deepak didn't expect it.

Slayne drew a gun.

Seattle

Ben Thomas stood with his hands on his hips and stared at the vehicle being loaded into his trailer. "What is that thing? I've never seen anything like it."

McDermott didn't look up from his clipboard. "It's a

special order. A custom job for some nutcase movie director. I guess for one of his movies. He calls it a SEAL."

"A what?"

"You know. Those animals with flippers that balance balls on their noses."

McDermott scribbled something and regarded the vehicle with amusement. "SEAL is a—what do you call it when each letter stands for a word?"

"An acronym."

"How the hell did you know that?"

Ben took slight offense. "What? I must be dumb because I'm black?"

"No, no, that's not what I meant. Damn. How long have we known each other and you say a thing like that?" McDermott shook his head. "Anyway, SEAL is a—whatever you called it—for Solar-Energized Amphibious or Land recreational vehicle."

"It doesn't look recreational to me," Ben observed. "It looks like something the army would use."

McDermott glanced around as if to make sure no one was close enough to overhear, then leaned toward Ben and whispered, "You didn't get this from me, but there's a rumor the thing is fitted out like a tank. With real weapons and all."

"You're kidding."

"It's just what I was told. I've love to take a peek inside, but the doors are locked and I'm under orders not to. You'll notice we're not driving it into the trailer. We're winching it."

"I wondered about that." Ben was wondering about a few other things, as well. "Movie director, you say?"

"Yep. Some guy who's made a lot of scary movies and action flicks." McDermott tapped the clipboard. "I've got his name right here. Carpenter. Kurt Carpenter."

"I've seen most of his movies." Ben rattled a few titles off. "Is that the guy we're talking about?"

"I wouldn't know the titles. But I bet the weapons this thing is supposed to have are fake."

"I bet you're right." Ben's phone beeped and he answered it, but couldn't hear for all the noise. Covering his other ear, he said loudly, "Hold on!" Then he moved toward the opposite corner of the warehouse, where nothing was going on. "Who is this again?"

"Becca Levy, Mr. Thomas. Are you on your way yet?"

"Not yet, no. Your package is being loaded right now." Ben paused. "Why didn't you tell me you work for Kurt Carpenter? When you called, you said you were with some outfit called Home Enterprises."

"Mr. Carpenter has many business interests. H.E. is one of them." Her tone became concerned. "How soon can you leave Seattle?"

"I won't get out of here for half an hour yet."

"I'll be candid, Mr. Thomas. We're worried. Very worried. The SEAL is crucial to Mr. Carpenter's plans. It was supposed to have been delivered six months ago, but a few design flaws had to be worked out. It's a prototype, you see. That means there's no other like it anywhere in the world."

"I know what prototype means."

"It's almost seventeen hundred miles from Seattle to Lake Bronson State Park. Yet you honestly believe you can make it here in forty-eight hours?"

"Less if I don't have any problems."

"I would expect problems, Mr. Thomas. We're on the verge of World War Three. Much of the Middle East and north Africa are in flames. Beirut is gone. Tel Aviv has been vaporized. In the United States, all contact has been lost with San Diego. There are reports of foreign troops in

Canada, pushing south. Riots and looting have broken out. Martial law is to be imposed nationwide at ten AM tomorrow."

"Forty-eight hours or less," Ben insisted.

"You're very sure of yourself."

"I was a U.S. Marine, lady. The few. The proud. The kickass. You're paying me three times the going rate to get your fancy rig to you and that's exactly what I'm going to do."

"I hope so. Be careful, Mr. Thomas." Becca Levy hung up.

Ben shoved the phone into his pocket. He considered her last words. On an impulse, he went to a metal ladder and climbed to the catwalk. Wire mesh covered the window, but he could see out. And what he saw sent a shiver down his spine.

The Space Needle and the rest of Seattle's skyline were as they always were: futuristic, imposing, impressive. But sirens blared and police and ambulance lights flashed everywhere. Smoke curled skyward from a score of locations. The crackle of what sounded like firecrackers wasn't firecrackers at all; it was gunfire.

Ben hurried down and over to his truck. He climbed into the cab of the truck he'd named Semper Fi and did another run-through. Earlier he'd topped off his fuel tank and had the engine serviced. Diesel, oil, coolant, tires, all had been checked and rechecked. Once he cranked over the engine, he could be on his way.

A fist pounded on the door.

"I need your John Hancock," McDermott said, and held up the clipboard with forms for him to sign. "We're about done. Five minutes and you're good to go."

Ben unclipped a pen from his shirt pocket. "Can you

believe what is going down out there?" he asked with a nod at the high windows.

"It's crazy, is what it is. One of the guys was just telling me that an enemy sub had been sighted in Puget Sound."

"Which enemy?"

"Damned if I know. I doubt he did, either. Probably just another rumor. Reminds me of World War Two, when people were seeing Japanese subs all over the place and blowing fish out of the water." McDermott shook his head. "It's a mad world out there and getting madder by the moment."

Ben handed back the clipboard and slid the pen into his pocket. Turning in the driver's seat, he made sure his duffel bag was there. He patted it, saying, "I can't leave without my babies."

"Did you hear something?"

Suddenly the building shook to a concussive blast. The windows rattled so hard, several cracked.

"What the hell?" McDermott blurted. "That was an explosion."

"I need to go."

McDermott nodded. "I'll hurry things along." He ran toward the rear of the trailer.

Ben switched on the radio to an all-news station.

"Citizens are being advised to remain indoors. The streets aren't safe. Unruly mobs are on the loose. Gun stores have been broken into. People are taking food and water from stores without paying. The police report that outside agitators are at work, but they haven't explained exactly what they mean by that."

The announcer took a breath.

"Incredible as it sounds, our social structure is breaking down. It has become every man, every woman, for him or herself."

He paused.

"In other news, Turkey, Italy, and Greece are now embroiled in the spreading conflict, which the secretary-general of the United Nations has described as the beginning of the end for Western civilization unless world leaders can agree on an immediate ceasefire. England and France are mobilizing troops, while in . . ."

Ben turned off the radio. He nearly jumped at another pounding on his door. "What?"

"Geez. Bite my head off, why don't you?" McDermott smiled. "You're good to go, buddy."

The warehouse reverberated to Semper Fi's roar.

Rollers squeaking, the bay doors rattled open.

Ben Thomas shifted into gear, put the pedal to the metal, and rumbled out into madness.

Tangled Webs

Minnesota

The drawbridge was down. Kurt Carpenter had called ahead and they were ready for him. As Holland drove the long black limousine along the dirt track that was their only link to civilization, Carpenter peered ahead and nodded in satisfaction.

His brainchild was a thirty-acre compound surrounded by twenty-foot-high brick walls. Aqueducts at the northwest and southeast corners diverted a stream into an inner moat, a secondary line of defense should the brick walls ever be breached.

The limo didn't stop once it was across the moat. Holland made for the closest of six concrete bunkers. C Block, Carpenter had designated it, where the Communications Center was housed.

Becca Levy was waiting. As always, she was smartly dressed. She spoke into a wafer-thin mouthpiece attached to an ear jack in her left ear. She stopped talking as he emerged from the backseat of the limo, and she held out her hand for him to shake. "Good to see you made it, boss."

"Give me a breakdown."

"Twenty-seven are here already. We expect another forty-one to show up in the next eight hours."

"And the rest?"

"They're aware of the deadline. They know what it means if they don't make it."

Carpenter strode toward the entrance to C Block, Becca keeping up with his brisk pace. "Any word on the SEAL?"

"The transporter was just leaving Seattle the last time I spoke to him."

"I'm counting on him. The SEAL is my gift to those who come after us. Provided we survive, that is." Carpenter stopped and scanned the compound. Two men with rifles were on the west wall near the drawbridge. To the east were trees and a row of cabins. Beyond that were fields he planned to devote to tilling. "God. I hope I've covered every contingency. One mistake, and we'll be no better off than those pour souls caught in the cities."

"You've done a remarkable job, sir. You have every reason to be proud."

Carpenter entered C Block. The Com Center boasted the best equipment his money could buy, all of it state-of-the-art, complete with satellite linkups and GPS. A large screen was flagged with dots, one for every person Carpenter had selected. "Many of them have a long way to come."

"We estimate a 97 percent success ratio," Becca Levy reported. "Provided that most of them are clear of the major population centers before the missiles start to fly."

"What's the latest on the war front?"

"The United States has responded to the nuking of its Mediterranean Task Force with strategic nuclear strikes against two Middle Eastern countries. China has denounced that as an act of war. Chinese and North Korean forces have been mobilized."

Carpenter sadly shook his head. "It's only a matter of time before one of our cities is taken out. That will be the beginning of the end."

"Not for us," Becca said. "You've stocked enough provisions to last a thousand years. The Blocks are reinforced to withstand everything except a direct nuclear strike. We're not near any city or prospective military target. We'll be just fine."

"You don't understand, Ms. Levy. Yes, I expect we'll survive. That's the whole point behind the millions I've invested in this project. But what then?"

"Sir?"

"The world as we know it is about to come to an end. My experts inform me that the mix of nuclear, chemical, and biological weapons will wreak havoc with our planet."

"Need I remind you, sir, that the world survived all those test bombs and the bombs that were dropped on Japan?"

"This time there won't be a dozen nuclear explosions over twenty years. There might be hundreds, and all that radiation will interact with the chemical and biological agents, with unforeseen results. Mutations will be the norm, not the exception. Creatures and conditions we can't begin to imagine."

"You make it sound like nothing will ever be the same again."

"It won't."

Philadelphia

"I don't want trouble," Soren Anderson said while easing his right hand around his tool belt.

The five gangstas spread out. Four held knives. The fifth

had a blackjack. The tall one crouched and came toward Soren, who balanced on the balls of his feet.

"Give us the keys, man. Don't make us do you."

"I can't. I have a family. I must get to them." Soren's fingers closed on the handle of his ball-peen hammer. "Leave me be or I'll hurt you."

"Can't count, can you, sucker?"

The tall one nodded at two others. They came at Soren in a rush. He waited until the last possible instant, until the quicker of the pair thrust a blade at him. Then, sidestepping, Soren whipped his hammer out and around. He was a big man and it was a big hammer. It weighed three pounds; the head alone was thirty-six ounces. Drop-forged and heat-treated, it made for a formidable weapon.

Soren caught the gangsta on the temple. There was a *crunch* of bone yielding to metal and the youth dropped at Soren's feet, convulsing violently.

The second gangsta barely slowed. Swearing viciously, he lunged at Soren's groin. He was so focused on Soren that he tripped over his fallen friend. Before he could recover, Soren swept the hammer against his skull.

The remaining three stood rooted in disbelief. Then the tall one snarled, "Get him, yo!"

All three came at Soren at once.

Backpedaling, Soren swung the ball-peen hammer from side to side to keep them at bay. They weren't eager to share the fate of their friends and held back. But it was only a matter of time before one of them would bloody his blade. They knew it, and Soren knew it. Which was why Soren did what he did. *He* charged *them*.

They were caught flat-footed. Only the tall one turned to flee. Soren clipped one and sent him reeling, then smashed another in the face and dropped him in his tracks. A couple of long bounds and he caught up to the tall one, who shrieked and thrust his knife at Soren's throat. A flick of Soren's other hand, and he had hold of the gangsta's wrist.

"You should have let me go, boy."

"Please, mister!"

Soren swung a last time. He stood with his chest heaving, more from excitement than the exertion, and regarded the blood and gore smeared on the hammer. "So this is what it feels like."

The wail of a siren reminded Soren where he was. He ran to his pickup, unlocked the door, and climbed in. He set the hammer on the seat beside him. Gunning the engine, he made for the exit. The construction site bordered Seventh Street. He turned right, intending to get to 676 and take it west to 76. The first intersection he came to was South Street.

Slamming on his brakes, Soren gaped. Vehicles were bumper to bumper and door to door. People were cursing, shouting, shaking fists. A policeman was trying to get traffic moving again, but all of his whistle blowing and arm waving was in vain.

Soren shifted into reverse. No cars were behind him yet and he didn't want to be boxed in. Placing his arm across the top of the seat, he twisted and backed up until he came to an alley. Wheeling the pickup bed into it, he spun the steering wheel and drove in the other direction.

Soren did some fast thinking. Based on what he had seen from atop the skyscraper and just now, Philly's major arteries were a mess. It would take forever to get out of the city. His best bet, he reasoned, was to stick to side streets and alleys.

For over an hour that was what he did. Finally he made it onto 676. Traffic was at a snail's pace. Fuming with frustration, he crawled toward the expressway. His frustration was compounded by worry for his family. Eight times he tried to call his wife. Eight times he got a busy signal.

Soren merged onto 76. He was able to go fifty now, which was still too slow to suit him. He got out his phone, pressed a button, and nearly whooped with happiness when at long last it rang at the other end.

"Hello?"

"Toril!" Soren tingled with relief. He envisioned her golden hair, the lake blue of her eyes, the body he knew almost as well as he knew his own. "Are you and the kids all right? I've been trying to get through."

"My mother called. I couldn't get her off. She's scared, Soren. Very scared. She says military convoys have been going by all day."

Soren's mother-in-law lived outside of Harrisburg on a hill overlooking Interstate 81.

"The National Guard is being mobilized. There's talk of sending more troops to the Middle East."

"*That* has her scared?"

"She heard on the radio that gas and food will be rationed. And that the Chinese or the Russians have a new biological weapon they're threatening to use if we don't recall our forces already deployed."

"Which is it?"

"What?"

"The Chinese or the Russians."

"She couldn't remember."

Soren smothered a sigh. He liked his mother-in-law. She was a dear lady. But she'd had Toril late in life—at age forty—and now the old woman was pushing eighty and her faculties were impaired. Which was putting it delicately.

"Soren, I've heard gunfire."

"Shots? Where?"

"Not far off. Freya is scared to go outside. Magni wants

to, but I won't let him. I have them both down in the basement." Toril paused. "Soren, what is going on? The news makes it sound like the country is falling apart."

The worry in her voice was an icy fist around Soren's heart. "I'm on my way. Get down in the basement with the kids, bolt the door, and stay there until I get home."

"How long will that be?" Toril asked anxiously.

"I wish I could say." Soren had more he wanted to tell her but a dial tone filled his ear. He punched his home number and got another busy signal. Figuring that his wife was trying to call him, he hung up and waited. His phone didn't beep. He let several minutes go by, then impatiently tried her again. Yet another busy signal.

Soren almost threw his phone out the window. When he needed it most, modern technology failed him. He supposed he should be grateful he had gotten through at all. He'd read about something called an EMP effect, and that if a nuclear weapon was detonated at high altitude over the center of the United States, an electromagnetic pulse would wipe out electronic equipment from the Atlantic to the Pacific.

Soren prayed that wouldn't happen. If the panic was bad now, he couldn't imagine how bad it would become if every phone and computer in the country were suddenly useless.

The driver of the car in front of him applied its brakes. Soren did the same. Beyond the car was a long line of stalled vehicles. A traffic jam, he speculated. He hated this. He needed to be with his family.

A secondary road paralleled 76 on his side of the highway. Hardly any vehicles were using it. But to reach it, he'd have to go over a cement barrier, down an embankment, and up the other side. He thought of the money he had invested in having the pickup body jacked up and in buying the largest tires it could handle. Spinning the wheel, he nosed up to the barrier. Someone shouted and a horn blared but he ignored them. His front tires made contact, and he braked. Then, mentally crossing his fingers, he gunned the 367-horsepower Vortec Max 6.OL V8 engine. The front of his pickup leaped skyward, and for a few awful seconds he thought the truck would flip over. He bounced so hard, the seat belt dug into his gut. Then it was the rear end that tilted toward the sky, and a moment later he was roaring down the embankment. He slewed up onto the road and turned west.

"Honey, here I come," Soren said out loud.

Phoenix

Shock riveted Professor Diana Trevor to the wing of her plane. But only until Harry Pierce's fingers closed on her throat and his other hand grabbed at her keys.

Diana reacted without thinking. She raked her hand down Pierce's face, drawing blood with her nails. He shrieked and jerked his head back, and she kicked him where kicking a man always did the most good.

Gurgling and sputtering, Harry sat down hard on his backside on the tarmac and clutched himself.

"What the hell was that?" Diana snapped.

Red in the face and shuddering from pain, Harry rasped, "I told you I need to get to Kansas City."

"And I told you that's too far out of my way." Diana turned to her cockpit. "If you're still sitting there after I've turned her over, I'll run right over you. I swear to God."

The last she saw of him, he was hobbling stiff-legged toward the hangar.

Diana busied herself with the preflight checklist. She removed the control wheel lock and turned the master switch on. She checked the fuel. She turned the lights on and off. She moved the flaps and the ailerons. She climbed back out of the cockpit, took off the rudder gust lock, and removed the tail tie-down. She didn't have time to do a complete empennage check but she did go to the nose and made sure the air intakes were open.

Presently, Diana was strapped in and ready. She tried to raise the tower but no one responded. "What on earth is going on?" she asked the empty air, then decided she wouldn't wait around twiddling her thumbs.

What she was about to do was against all the rules, but Diana didn't care. She needed to reach the compound, and she would do whatever it took to get there.

Another five minutes found her on the runway ready for takeoff. She slowly advanced the throttle and just as slowly pulled back on the yoke. Her nose climbed, her wheels lifted, and she was airborne.

She was tempted to circle the city, but every minute was crucial. The missiles might fly while she was in the air, and even if she wasn't near an impact zone, an EMP or concussive ripple might knock her out of the air.

At seven thousand feet Diana leveled off. She listened to the radio for a while. It was confusion times ten. A near-hysterical announcer declared that the West Coast had been attacked, but he didn't say where or by whom and the signal gave way to static. Another said that federal resources had been strained to the point of collapse. A parson on a religious station intoned that the end times were upon them.

Diana realized her palms were sweating and wiped them on her pants. She had a long flight ahead of her. She put the plane on autopilot. Then she opened her briefcase and took out a laptop and a disc marked Endworld. She got the computer running and inserted the disc. Scrolling down the contents screen, she clicked on a file labeled Correspondence w/ Carpenter. A list of letters, e-mails and dates appeared. She clicked on the letter she wanted.

Dr. Trevor,

It is with the greatest satisfaction that I can inform you of the results of your screening. You have passed the physical and background check with impressive scores. I feel you will make a most worthy addition to the enterprise I am undertaking.

You posed a few questions when last we talked on the phone. I didn't have the time to go as deeply into detail as I would have liked, so now I'll remedy that.

The idea for a survivalist retreat first came to me seven years ago. There have always been wars and rumors of wars. Despite the global conflicts that took such terrible tolls in lives lost, I became convinced the worst was yet to come. A proverbial "war to end all wars," as it were. To put it more frankly, I became so cynical as to not put any stupidity past the human race—and that included another world war.

With me to think is to act. So I put into motion the plan that has resulted in the compound you visited, and my grand scheme to salvage something worthwhile from the ruin of modern civilization.

I'm not boasting when I state that I've amassed a considerable fortune from my movies. I used some of it on research and development of what I came to call the Endworld Protocol. I needed to find an isolated spot as far from military and civilian targets as feasible. The property near Lake Bronson State Park is ideal.

Construction of the compound came next, and I don't need to tell you how costly that proved.

I refused to skimp. The concrete bunkers—the Blocks, as I call them—are architectural marvels. Each is a self-contained survival habitat. Barring a direct strike, they should withstand any calamity to come.

Next was the step that proved most daunting: finding those I'd invite to come live in my new Eden once war broke out. I consulted experts in every field. It was at this phase that I came into contact with you, principally due to your studies in the field of dominance as it involves human personalities and societal interaction.

That was when another idea occurred to me. The brave new world I envisioned demanded a brave new type of person to adapt and thrive. The key, as I saw it, was to find people who embody that dominant factor you have written and lectured about. Imagine, if you will, a group where the ratio isn't one in twenty—but a group where everyone is a dominant personality. Some would call that an invitation to friction and disaster. I believe it will result in a group dynamic that will enable us to perform beyond all expectations.

This is where the test you have developed for identifying dominant personalities will prove invaluable.

There was more but Diana went back to the list, scrolled down farther, and clicked on an e-mail. She was particularly interested in certain paragraphs.

You expressed amusement when I told you some of the finer details of exactly what I have planned.

"Hokey," I think, was the word you used, although to your credit you smiled when you said it.

But remember, we're dealing with a gathering of dominant personalities. By their very nature, they tend to be highly independent. They tend to do as they please and resist authority. We need a common bond for them to share, a sense of belonging that will knit them into a seamless whole.

The keys, as I see it, are the two basic building blocks of every social structure. Without them, few societies, few governments, last. For those I've invited to the compound to mesh as well as I want them to, they must be convinced of a commonality they share. That common thread is brotherhood.

I know, I know. You'll say I'm too much of an idealist. You'll say I'm not being practical. But I respectfully submit that unless we learn to work together as individuals, we won't survive as a group.

Diana would have read more, but the proximity alarm sounded. Startled, she looked up.

Another plane was on a collision course with hers.

Seattle

Ben Thompson could hardly believe it. The radio announcer was saying there were unconfirmed reports of a nuclear strike on San Diego. There were also sightings of enemy submarines off the West Coast. Add to that word from Canada that a large enemy force had pushed through Alaska into northern British Columbia, and it explained why Seattle had gone nuts.

The streets were a madhouse. Guns popped and crackled.

Screams pierced the air. Smoke spiraled toward storm clouds gathering overhead.

Ben hadn't counted on anything like this. But when he gave his word, he kept it. When he took a contract, he saw the contract through. Accordingly, when he came to the end of the block near the warehouse, he braked and opened his duffel bag. His babies lay on top.

When he had gotten his honorable discharge from the Marines, one of the first things he had done was buy a pair of Colt Double Eagles customized with nickel plating and wood grips instead of rubber. He was old school, and he liked the feel of wood under his fingers.

Ben took the pistols out of his duffel and placed them on the seat. A pair of clips was next. Then a box of .45 ACP ammo. With practiced skill he quickly fed cartridges into each magazine, then slapped a mag into each of the Double Eagles. He chambered rounds. Setting one pistol next to him, he wedged the other under his belt.

"I'm good to go."

Ben shifted and pulled out, the big rig sluggish until he got up to speed. The first few blocks were strangely deserted. Not a living soul in sight. Then he came to an intersection, started to turn, and slammed on the brakes.

Ahead was trouble. A man with a rifle was waving it at every vehicle. Drivers had stopped, some hunched over their steering wheels in what Ben took to be fear, as the man screamed and raved.

Ben had no idea what was going on but he couldn't afford a delay. He gave Semper Fi gas. The man heard him and raised his rifle. Ben waited until he was close enough to be sure and then braked. He smiled to give the impression he was friendly. His window was already down so all he had to do was lean out and holler, "What's going on, buddy?"

"I shot them and I'll shoot you if you're not careful!"

Ben looked at the stopped vehicles again, at the drivers hunched over their steering wheels, and a sick feeling came over him. Blood dripped from the chin of an elderly woman. A man had had one eye and part of its socket blown away. "Why?"

The man cackled. "Haven't you heard? It's the end of the world." And with that, he aimed his rifle at Ben.

A Pale Horse

New York City

Deepak Kapur was as astonished as everyone else when Patrick Slayne drew a pistol. Deepak had no idea what kind it was. His knowledge of firearms was limited to those he saw on TV and at the movies. Most of the time he had no idea what they were.

A woman was the first to find her voice. "Are you a policeman?"

"No." Slayne punched a button on the elevator panel.

"Then what gives you the right to tell us we can't take the elevator?" the same woman demanded.

Slayne wagged the pistol.

A man with thick sideburns shoved to the front. "I have half a mind to take that popgun away."

"You're right," Slayne said.

"I am?"

"You have half a mind."

The man took a half step, clearly tempted to try. But

then he locked eyes with Parick Slayne and something he saw made him step back and lower his fist.

The elevator arrived with a ping, and the door opened. Slayne beckoned to Deepak.

"Let's go. The streets will be a madhouse soon if they're not already. We must get out of the city before we're trapped here."

Deepak felt he had to say something to show his disapproval. "I can't say as I care much for your methods."

"My job is to get you to the compound any way I can. You're considered essential."

"No one told me."

The people cramming the hall started to mutter and whisper. Hostility was writ on nearly every face.

Slayne beckoned again. "If you please, Mr. Kapur. We don't have all night."

Reluctantly, Deepak started toward the elevator, only to be violently shoved by another man who tried to slip past. Slayne's arm moved too fast for Deepak to follow; there was the sound of a blow, and the man folded at the knees and sprawled onto the tiles, unconscious.

Some of the onlookers covered their mouths in shock. Deepak stared, aghast. He believed that violence was the last resort of those too feeble-minded to solve their problems a better way.

More muttering occurred. A big man shoved to the front and said in a loud, brave voice, "Are we going to let one guy stop us? Or haven't you heard that the news has been saying New York is going to be nuked?"

"Let's rush him!"

"I'm with you!"

Slayne pointed his pistol at the instigator. "If they try, you're the first one I'll shoot."

Deepak and everyone else heard a *click*. The brave man suddenly wasn't as brave and backed off.

"We're wasting time."

Slayne grabbed Deepak's wrist and pulled him toward the elevator. They were inside and the doors were starting to shut when Alf Richardson stuck a hand in front of one. Instantly, Slayne trained his pistol on Alf.

"Don't shoot me!"

"No!" Now it was Deepak who grabbed Slayne's wrist. "He's a friend of mine. He works in the same department. Let him come."

"Your call."

Deepak didn't know what to make of the man. He moved aside so Alf could join them.

Slayne stood barring the doors until they closed, then he pressed a button and the car pinged into motion.

"That wasn't the lobby you pressed," Alf said. "I need to get off at the lobby."

"We're not stopping until the underground garage."

"What is your problem?" Deepak came to Alf's aid. "Press the L and we'll let him out."

"No."

It was rare for Deepak to lose his temper. As a child in New Delhi, living on the raw edge of poverty, he had learned the importance of self-control. When his belly had been so empty it wouldn't stop hurting, he had learned to ignore it. When he had become so sick he couldn't stand up, he had learned to endure it. When he had been told by an uncle that he would never amount to much, he had quivered with the need to be someone. "You just said you'd do whatever I want."

"What *you* want to do," Slayne clarified. "Not what your friend wants to do."

"But what can it hurt?"

"A naval task force has been obliterated by a nuclear missile. There's a report San Diego has been hit. The National Guard is being called up, and the president is expected to go before Congress tomorrow and ask for a declaration of war." Slayne put a hand to his ear and seemed to listen intently.

"What are you doing?" Seepak had to know.

"Adjusting the frequency."

"The what?"

Slayne moved the hair that hung over his left ear, revealing an earpiece. "I'm listening to emergency services."

"You're sure full of tricks," Deepak said, and not by way of praise.

"It's my job."

"Cool," Alf said. "You're some kind of security guy, right? That's why you have the gun and stuff."

Slayne held up a hand for quiet. He was listening to his earpiece. "It's starting to unravel," he told Deepak.

"What is?"

"The infrastructure. People are on the verge of panic. They're being told to stay in their homes. But a lot of them don't have any food. Or they don't want to be trapped in the city when martial law is imposed. So an exodus is under way. New Yorkers are fleeing the city like rats fleeing a sinking ship."

"That doesn't sound good."

"Is that really how things are, mister?" Alf asked Slayne. "How will I get home? What will I do when I get there? I don't have much food, either."

The elevator pinged again and the doors hissed open. Rows of vehicles spread before them. Usually, the underground garage was orderly and peaceful. The only hectic moments were during the morning and evening rush hours. But now nearly everyone in the building who had a car was trying to leave at once, and the aisles were blocked.

Horns blared in a raucous din. Voices rose in the heat of anger.

"I was afraid of this," Patrick Slayne said.

"We should forget it and wait until things calm down," Deepak proposed. "Say, in half an hour or so."

Slayne looked at him. "You don't get it yet, Mr. Kapur. It will be a long time before things are ever *calm* again. This is the end of your world."

"What's he talking about?" Alf asked.

"Stay close," Slayne said, and he bore to the right. He passed several rows of vehicles. In one row, two men were swearing at each other over who had the right of way. In another, it was two women. Farther on, a car had backed into a station wagon and the owners were about to come to blows.

Alf uttered a nervous laugh. "Like I always say, there's a Neanderthal born every minute."

Deepak rose onto his toes. He could just see the exit ramp. It was crammed, many of the drivers leaning on their horns. "We'll never get out of here."

"That's what you think." Slayne hurried them down an aisle to where a black Hunster took up two parking spaces. Three times as large as an average car, with tires correspondingly huge, the Hunsters were a new line for those who didn't care about the cost of gas. Advertised as a "sportsman's dinosaur" in commercials that featured a gorgeous blonde in a French maid's uniform, they had been criticized by watchdog groups for their extravagant waste of fossil fuels.

"You've got to be kidding me," Deepak said.

Alf grinned like a kid in a candy shop. "I think it's awesome. If I could afford it, I'd have one of these monsters."

Patrick Slayne ignored them. He took a small remote

from his pocket and pressed a button. The Hunster burped and the driver's door popped open. "Get in," he said to Deepak. To Alf he said, "You're on your own."

"What? Wait. Can't I come with you? Only up to the street? Then you can let me out."

"No."

"Damn it, Slayne. What's the matter with you?" Deepak argued.

"He is not my responsibility. You are." Slayne began to climb inside.

"Well, I'm not going anywhere with you unless Alf gets to come, too."

Slayne sighed. "Fine," he relented. "We'll let him out on the street. But after that, he's on his own."

"Sweet," Alf said as he climbed into the back of the vehicle.

The driver's seat resembled a cockpit. Slayne flicked switches and pushed buttons and turned a key. The Hunster rumbled to mechanical life with a roar that shook the walls.

"T-Rex, move over!" Alf said. "Listen to this beast! I've died and gone to heaven."

"I didn't know you were into muscle cars," Deepak noted as he strapped himself in. He felt ridiculous sitting in a vehicle that was half as big as his apartment.

"Buddy, calling this a muscle car is like calling King Kong a monkey. This baby is a tank."

Slayne glanced back and the suggestion of a smile touched his lips. "I like the way you think." He had placed the pistol on the console, but now he picked it up and slid it between his legs.

"What on earth are you doing?" Deepak asked.

"I might need it quick." Slayne shifted into reverse and

backed out. He started toward the logjam at a crawl. Braking, he pressed a toggle switch. A loud whine came from underneath them and the Hunster began to rise.

"The hell!" Alf declared in delight.

"Hydraulics."

Slayne worked another toggle switch and after a few seconds there were *thunks* from the front and the rear.

Deepak couldn't resist. "What was that?"

"More hydraulics. The bumpers are realigning so I can use the battering ram."

"Did you say battering ram?"

Alf giggled.

Patrick Slayne touched his earpiece. "It's getting worse out there. Food riots have broken out. People are looting stores. There's a mob at the waterfront commandeering boats."

"Dude, you rock," Alf said.

Deepak was beginning to regret bringing him. "Don't encourage the man. I hardly know him."

Slayne put both hands on the steering wheel. "Hang on. And don't worry. The armor plating will protect us from small arms fire. But yell if you see a bazooka."

"You're kidding, right?" Deepak said. The next instant he was slammed against his seat as the Hunster accelerated. To his astonishment, they drove up on top of the car in front of them and from there to the top of the next. Metal bent. The occupants screeched and cursed.

Alf let out a hearty laugh from the backseat.

Lunging forward, Deepak grabbed Slayne by the shoulder. "What do you think you're doing? Stop! You'll hurt someone."

Slayne shrugged him off. "I need to concentrate."

"But you're *hurting* people."

"I'm doing my best not to crush anyone, but I've got to get you out of here." Slayne paused. "Besides, how do you feel about the two thousand and seventy-six people who died for you today?"

"What are you talking about?"

"The task force that was nuked. That's how many personnel were involved. Are you upset about them?"

"I didn't know them."

"You don't know these people, either." Slayne gunned the engine and drove over a pickup and into the next aisle. He made for the logjam nearest the ramp. But instead of slowing, he went faster.

"Please, no," Deepak pleaded. "I don't want any deaths on my conscience."

"Give me more credit. I'm not the heartless bastard you seem to think." Slayne spun the steering wheel. "Hang on!"

The Hunster bucked into the air and came down with a crash. It had cleared the first vehicle and started up the next. The crunch of metal was nearly continuous.

So were the oaths and yells.

Deepak glanced out the rear window. Somehow Slayne had managed to miss the drivers. Most were scrambling from their cars in terror. Without warning, Deepak's seat tried to achieve orbit, and he grabbed hold of the roll bar.

"This is so cool!" Alf cried.

For Deepak it was horrific. He realized that Slayne intended to take him cross-country. He could only imagine how much havoc they would wreak. It was a nightmare made real.

Then suddenly it became a whole lot worse.

For Love of Family

Philadelphia

The Trudale Subdivision was a gated community in the heart of Richter Downs. High walls, cameras, guards on duty every hour of the day and night, hourly patrols; Trudale was a secure island of well-to-do in a sea of squalor.

Richter Downs, however, was considered a blight on urban sprawl. Once a mix of residential and business zones, it had sunk into disrepair and disrepute. Gangs claimed the parks, drugs flooded the streets and the alleys, and law-abiding folk stayed behind locked doors at night. Poverty became its middle name.

Some critics thought building an oasis of wealth in the middle of so much want was asking for trouble. But the moneymen behind Trudale had confidence in their security force.

Soren Anderson had driven through Richter Downs a thousand times. It was the only way to reach Trudale. But he had never seen it like this. Normally, the streets were quiet if squalid. Kids threw balls or played on the sidewalks. Teens hung out on street corners looking tough. Oldsters sat on their stoops or in rocking chairs.

Today there were three times as many people as usual. A lot were listening to the latest news on radios. They cast scowls and glares his way. It didn't help that many were standing in the middle of the street, forcing Soren to use his horn to get through. Traffic, thankfully, was light, and had been since he'd left the freeway. Again and again, he'd tried to reach Toril. He suspected that the phone lines were so overloaded, it would be a wonder if he got through.

Soren turned onto Ballard Street. Ahead was the imposing gate that led into Trudale. Most days, few people were in the vicinity. The dilapidated buildings usually sat neglected and grim. Today Soren had to brake.

People were shoulder to shoulder in the street. The sidewalks were jammed. Where they had all come from, Soren couldn't imagine. Nor could he guess what they were all doing there. It seemed a strange place to come. He started forward and they got out of his way, but many gave him ugly looks, and one man flipped him the finger.

"What did I ever do?" Soren asked himself. He smiled at a woman holding two small children and she scowled.

Half a dozen uniformed guards were just inside the gate. In addition to the batons they carried, sidearms were strapped to their hips.

Captain Jeffors came out of the guard station and motioned for the gate to be opened. "Good afternoon, Mr. Anderson."

Soren pulled through the gate and stopped. "Any trouble?" he asked. "I haven't been able to get through to my wife."

"Everything is fine, sir," Jeffors said, but his tone and

the look he gave the lurkers outside the gate suggested otherwise.

"It's a madhouse in the city. I was lucky to make it out."

Captain Jeffors absently nodded while still staring at the people thronging Ballard Street. "You made it just in time. There's been talk on the news of closing down the city as soon as the Guard is brought in."

"How do you close down an entire city?" To Soren the idea was preposterous.

"By whatever means necessary," Jeffors said, then snapped his head up at the wail of a siren in the distance. "That one's an ambulance. Just a while ago it was the police."

The sound jarred Soren. "Well, I better be going. My family will be worried."

"Good luck, Mr. Anderson."

"Odin preserve you."

Captain Jeffors tore his gaze from the street. "Oh. That's right. You're the one they call the Norse nut." He smiled good-naturedly.

Soren could have explained that there was more to it than that. A lot more. He could have told Jeffors that to him the Norse gods were more than myth; they were his religion. But he didn't. It would only result in the same amused regard he was used to. He shifted his foot to the gas pedal and drove up the hill to Wyndemere Circle.

Three faces were pressed to the picture window. They were out the front door before he came to a stop in the driveway. Toril held back so he could hug Freya and Magni, then she was in his arms, warm and soft and smelling wonderful.

Soren had to swallow to speak. "I was so worried."

"So were we. There's been more shooting." Toril looked toward the far-off high fence. "Are we safe, Soren?"

"Why wouldn't we be?" Soren yearned to smother her

with kisses, but they were right out in the open and the kids were there. "Come on. Let's go in."

"I still can't reach Mother."

Soren held the door for them. He thought he heard a loud cry from the vicinity of the gate. He looked, although he couldn't see the gate for the intervening buildings. He listened, but the cry wasn't repeated.

"Did you forget something?" Toril asked.

"No." Soren closed the door and locked it. He followed them up the stairs to the living room. A picture window ran the length of one wall. Below spread the city. He liked the view. Most days it relaxed him. But today it filled him with unease. Or maybe it was the smoke and the sirens.

"I'm happy you came home early. The news makes it sound bad out there."

"It is."

Soren put his arm around Toril and she rested her cheek on his chest. For all of a minute they stood there, alone and complete and safe. Then, faint but unmistakable, came the sound of a scream, and Soren shook himself and straightened. "There's something you need to know."

"You look so serious. What can it be?"

Soren told her everything. How he had seen an ad in the back of *Popular Mechanics*. Someone needed skilled craftsmen. The pay was a one-time lump sum. A *large* sum. The specific job wasn't mentioned. Dollar signs floating in his head, Soren answered the ad. To his surprise, he was sent a psychological exam, as well as an application form. He filled them out and sent them in. To his greater surprise, about ten weeks later he was notified by certified mail that he had been selected.

Soren met in Philadelphia with a woman named Becca Levy. She apologized for the secrecy, then dropped the bombshell that she worked for Kurt Carpenter, the famous filmmaker, and that Carpenter had constructed a survivalist compound in the wilds of northern Minnesota and was looking to invite people to live there, should the unthinkable become real.

"Not just anybody," Becca Levy had said. "Only special people who fit special needs. People like you, Mr. Anderson."

Soren had asked the question uppermost on his mind. "When will we be paid the money promised in the ad?"

Levy had produced a checkbook. "I'm authorized to disburse funds once you've signed our standard contract."

Now, standing at the picture window with his wife, Soren gazed down at the driveway. "That's how I was able to afford the truck."

"And you never told me?"

The hurt in her tone cut Soren deeply. "I never thought anything would come of it. I honestly never really expected there would be another world war."

"So what now?"

Before Soren could answer, Freya called out from the far corner where she and Magni were watching TV.

"Mom! Dad! You need to come see this."

Soren clasped Toril's hand and went over. Both children were on their bellies on the wood floor. On the flat screen a visibly shaken announcer had paused to collect himself.

"What is it?" Soren asked.

"He just said—" Freya began, but stopped when the newsman started to speak.

> *"I repeat. This just in. There have been three nuclear attacks on the West Coast. San Diego, San Francisco, and Portland have been hit. The footage you are about to see is from San Diego. We warn our viewers this will be deeply disturbing to watch."*

The scene displayed San Diego as captured on video from somewhere east of the city. The bright sun, the blue of the bay speckled with boats, the gleaming skyscrapers, the streets and flow of traffic were all normal and peaceful. The person who had taken the video was talking, but the voice had been muted. Suddenly the scene erupted in a spectacular flash of light. With stunning swiftness, a mushroom cloud formed, rising in the sky. The boats, the buildings, the cars, the people, all were obliterated in a span of heartbeats.

Soren felt Toril's nails dig into his flesh. His mouth went dry, and he had to try several times to swallow. He couldn't believe what he was seeing. But it had happened, really happened.

The newscaster came back on. He was as pale as paper.

"No word yet on fatalities. Communications along much of the West Coast and as far east as Utah have been disrupted. As yet we don't know if these were missiles or bombs or possibly backpack nukes planted by terrorists."

The man paused.

"Ladies and gentlemen, we have just received word that the president is about to announce a declaration of war. We expect to switch to our Washington bureau in a few minutes for the announcement. In the meantime, people are urged to stay in their homes and to stay calm. Contrary to rumors, there are no reports of enemy troops on U.S. soil. Stay tuned to this channel for breaking developments as they occur."

Soren had heard enough. "I want all of you to pack whatever you want to take. We're leaving in ten minutes."

"Leaving?" Freya said in surprise.

"Where are we going?" Magni asked.

"I'll tell you all about it on the way. Right now it's important you do exactly as I say and go pack." Soren struggled to keep his voice calm. How did he explain to a twelve-year-old and an eight-year-old that Armageddon had been let loose, and their world would never be the same?

"My mother?" Toril said.

Soren nodded. "We'll pick her up on the way." He shooed the kids off to their rooms, then went to the stairs and down to his workshop. It occurred to him that he needed a weapon. He didn't own a firearm. Toril disliked guns and wouldn't allow one in the house.

Soren didn't mind. He wasn't into guns, anyway. As a believer in the Ancient Way, he had long been fascinated by the weapons of the gods. In particular, he was intrigued by the weapon of his favorite, the god he most admired, the god he worshipped as truly and really as his neighbors worshipped Jesus or the Moslems worshipped Mohammed or the Buddhists revered Gautama.

On a wall of the workshop hung a sword, a shield, a dagger, and a mace. All were reproductions of actual Norse weaponry.

But it was the weapon in a position of honor at the center of the wall that Soren took down and held in his big hands. It was a replica of Mjolnir, the hammer wielded by Thor, the God of Thunder. Soren smiled as he held it up to the light.

"Crusher," he said fondly.

The short handle was made of lignum vitae, one of the hardest woods known to man, and wrapped in leather strips. The head had been forged of high carbon, heat-treated steel, cast in a mold. It was an exact copy of a Mjolnir on display at the Swedish Museum of National Antiquities.

Soren swung it a few times, his muscles rippling. It was as heavy as a sledgehammer and required great strength to wield. Toril had bought it for him as a gift years ago. Knowing how much it had cost, he had been in shock for days afterward. He kept telling her she shouldn't have, but the truth was, he had been delighted beyond measure.

Soren glanced at the other weapons. The sword was too long and heavy for Toril. The dagger, though, might be of use. He took it down and hastened upstairs to the living room. The others were in the bedrooms, getting ready. He paused in front of the TV.

> *". . . asking all citizens to remain calm. The United States military is on full alert. The National Guard has been mobilized. Police forces and sheriff departments are coordinating with state and federal officials to ensure our streets are safe. Stay in your homes. Stay off the phone unless in an emergency."*

Toril was throwing clothes into an open suitcase on the bed when Soren walked in. She ran a hand through her hair and said in mild exasperation, "I need more time. I can't seem to think straight. You said this place is in Minnesota, right? Should I go into storage and get some of our winter clothes?"

"It's the middle of the summer," Soren teased, and then saw her eyes. Setting Mjolnir on the bed, he took her in his arms. She pressed her forehead to his chest and trembled.

"I'm sorry. I'm scared, Soren. I'm worried about Mother, and I'm worried about us." Toril looked up, her eyes brimming with tears. "Most of all I'm worried about Freya and Magni. They're our *children*, Soren. They shouldn't have to go through this."

"No one should," Soren said. He held her close, her body warm against his, his heart filled near to bursting.

Magni dashed into the bedroom, yelling, "Dad! Mom! Come quick! There are people outside. People all over."

Soren grabbed Mjolnir. His long legs brought him to the picture window ahead of the others. Freya was there, horror on her face. He looked down, and his skin crawled.

Trudale had been breached. Defying all reason, the mob had broken through the gate and was running amok through the development. Residents were being attacked, car windshields smashed, windows hit with bottles and rocks. Down the block several men threw their shoulders against a door and it buckled. As they disappeared inside, a woman screamed.

Toril's hand found Soren's arm. "What do we do? What happens when they reach our house?"

Even as she spoke, half a dozen human wolves came bounding up Wyndemere Circle.

Aerial Roulette

Arizona Airspace

To Dr. Diana Trevor, the seconds it took to disengage the autopilot were eternities of dread. The plane bearing down on her was an older Beechcraft. She couldn't imagine why the other pilot didn't realize their peril. She went to dive out of danger when the other plane sheered off, passing uncomfortably close to her wing. She tried to call it on the radio. Angry, she watched it dwindle in the distance until it was a speck in the sky.

Diana returned to the routine of her flight. She had a long way to go. Her flight plan called for stops at small private airfields where she was less likely to run into the problems she foresaw for the larger public fields once panic set in. She'd worked it out in meticulous detail and was confident she would reach Minnesota, barring the unforeseen.

The reports on the airwaves painted a disturbing image. The attack on the task force had shattered any complacency people felt about the onset of the conflict in the Middle East. For more than a century there had been minor wars and terrorist attacks and political upheavals; this time it was all or nothing, the war to end all others.

On Diana flew.

Eventually Arizona was behind her. She made it across Colorado. Each stop was routine. She stayed well away from large cities like Colorado Springs and Denver.

The news reports grew more and more alarming. Panic was spreading. People were beginning to realize that things they took for granted wouldn't necessarily be available. Simple things, such as where their next meal was coming from. The illusion of security was being shattered.

Diana had long wondered why so many of her fellow citizens took so much for granted. They assumed that filling their bellies would always be easy, that the corner grocery would always be open and their favorite fast-food outlets or restaurants would always have food for the buying. They assumed they could always get fuel for their vehicles. They assumed the police would always be a phone call away, ready to serve and protect. Now they were learning the depths of their delusions.

Civilization was a house of cards. Knock away one card and the entire house came undone, collapsing in on itself of its own pretensions. That was her opinion, anyway, and it was a view Kurt Carpenter shared.

Diana made it to Nebraska. Flying over the state stirred memories of her childhood. She had been born and raised in Elkhorn, outside Omaha. Her childhood had been apple pie and Sunday school. Her parents had been surprised when she announced that she intended to enlist in the navy after high school. They didn't understand her desire to see something of the world.

Her hitch had opened her eyes. She had served onboard a destroyer that called at various Pacific ports. Some—Australia, for instance—were a lot like home. Others—

Southeast Asia—showed her how wretched human existence could be. She saw people living in abject misery. People so malnourished, they were literally skin and bone. She saw children swim in water contaminated by human feces. She saw bodies left to rot.

Diana had realized a great truth. Life owed no one a living. Life owed no one their next meal, or a roof over their head, or even the clothes on their back. Life owed them nothing but *life*. The rest was up to them to procure any way they could.

So-called basic human rights were not part of the natural order. A person wasn't born with the inherent right to free speech. A man-made document made that possible. The "right" was as flimsy as the paper it was written on.

After her navy stint, Diana had used the GI Bill to attend college. She had majored in psychology because the human mind fascinated her. Not so much how it worked as the delusions it fostered. Its capacity to deceive itself was boundless.

Diana had become interested in how the mind and its beliefs affected personality. That had led her to her research on dominance, which, in turn, led Kurt Carpenter to her. And here she was, on her way to his compound, hoping to ride out the end of the world in one of the few places on earth designed to do just that.

Diana smiled, thinking of how nice it would be to see Kurt again. She reached for her thermos.

And her plane died.

The Boena bucked as if hit by a gust of wind. The electronics blipped out and the props stopped spinning. Far to the west, a strange luminosity lit the sky. There was no sound other than the shear of wind as the Boena dipped and began to lose altitude.

Diana fought down a spike of fear. She knew what to

do in a situation like this. She still had control, limited control, but there was every chance she could bring the plane in for a safe landing. She was over western Nebraska, somewhere in the vicinity of North Platte. The country below was mostly farmland. Nebraska had never suffered from a lack of flat ground, so she should be able to find a spot to set down.

Flying a plane without power was a lot like driving a car without power. It took concentration and strength and iron nerves.

Diana banked slightly and peered out of the cockpit. She needed a field or a road or highway. Patchwork squares of farmland grew in size. A green patch became corn and a yellow patch became oats. A ribbon of brown was a dusty country road.

She decided to try for the road. A straight stretch looked long enough. There were no cars or trucks. Provided she didn't hit a rut or pothole, she should be able to bring in her bird.

Her angle of descent was just right. She aligned the plane with the middle of the road and braced for the bump of her wheels setting down. She was so intent on the road that she didn't pay much attention to the fences on each side.

She landed perfectly. She was moving fast, but she had plenty of space. Already she was thinking of what she would do when she got out. Too late, she saw a dip that ran the width of the road. The nose dropped, there was a shriek of mangled metal, the plane bounced, and then it slowed and went into a spin.

Diana had fleeting glimpses of sky and field and road. The Boena hit the fence and she heard metallic twangs that reminded her of guitar strings being plucked. A pole loomed, and she shrank into her seat and covered her head with her arms. The impact jarred her. Her tail rose and she thought the plane would flip over, but it crashed back down.

Then all was still.

Diana lowered her arms. The plane was in a ditch. The broken pole lay over a partly crumpled wing. Strands of wire were tangled everywhere. But she was alive. She unstrapped herself and climbed out, then stood on the wing and sniffed. She didn't smell fuel.

The blue sky mocked her. She turned in a circle. All she saw was farmland. Not a building anywhere. To the north were low hills.

Diana tried the radio, but it wouldn't work. Nothing would. EMP effect, was her guess. She got her backpack and her bottle of water and out of habit reached for her laptop. Without power it was a piece of junk. She wouldn't lose anything essential, though; it was all backed up on disc, and the discs were in her pack.

The ground felt spongy after so much flying. Diana hopped up and down a few times, then headed north along the road. She didn't look back. Her past was behind her in more ways than one.

She hadn't gone far when movement in a belt of trees between fields alerted her to wildlife. She expected deer, but instead saw two coyotes staring back at her.

Usually, coyotes weren't dangerous. But Diana shrugged out of her backpack. At the top was the last item she had packed: mace. She hefted it, thinking it was too bad it had been in her backpack when Harold Pierce had come at her. She would have loved to spray him smack in the eyes.

Diana looked up. The coyotes were gone. She stuck the mace in her front pocket, slid her shoulders into her backpack, and set off down the road, seeking a sign of habitation.

It was a gorgeous sunny day. The temperature was pushing ninety-five but she didn't mind the heat. She never had. It was cold that got to her.

She admired the fine blue of the sky and the puffy white of the clouds, and reflected on the irony that on the other side of the world, at that very moment, the sky was choked with radioactive dust.

Diana wondered how far the EMP effect reached. She wondered, too, with rising concern, how she was going to get from Nebraska to Minnesota before the deadline.

Kurt Carpenter had a timetable. Those he selected had exactly one hundred hours from the moment the first nukes detonated on U.S. soil to reach the compound. And that was the best-case scenario. As Carpenter had put it to her, "I can't jeopardize the welfare of the majority for the sake of a few. Our only hope of weathering the worst of it is to hunker in our bunkers and stay there until the radiation levels drop."

A hundred hours was a lot of time. Diana could make it to Minnesota by car, provided she could get her hands on one. But they looked to be scarce in this particular part of the heartland.

Diana had hiked for about ten minutes when the growl of an engine reached her. She questioned how that could be with the EMP effect. Then she remembered. The pulse fried electronic systems in use. Those not being used—a car that wasn't running, for instance—weren't affected.

She moved to the side of the road and waited.

The source of the growl came over a low rise ahead of her. It was a pickup, an antique popular in her great-grandfather's day, spewing as much smoke as noise. Clunking and rattling, it bore down on her at a turtle crawl. Then gears ground and the pickup leaped toward her like an old tiger eager to sink its fangs into fresh prey.

Diana smiled and waved.

In a swirl of dust and a belch of exhaust, the pickup came to a stop next to her. The driver had to be in his sixties if he was a day. He wore a grimy T-shirt with holes in it and jeans so thin it was a wonder his leg hairs didn't poke through.

He grinned, revealing yellow teeth, where he had teeth. He also had a lazy eye that tended to drift. "How do, girlie? Was it you in that plane I saw come down from my barn?"

"Afraid so," Diana confirmed. "Any chance you can give me a lift to the next town?"

The old man snickered. "Dearie, that would take an hour or better. And the radio's been saying as how we should stick close to home on account of the invasion."

"What invasion?"

"Haven't you heard? There's talk the Chinese army is pushing down from Canada and the Russians are set to land in Philadelphia."

"That's preposterous."

The old man reached across and pushed the passenger door open. It creaked on long-neglected hinges. "Come to my place and you can hear it yourself."

The man was nice enough, and it would be stupid of her to stay there when he was offering her a lift. She shrugged out of her backpack, placed it on the floor, and climbed in. The door creaked even louder when she slammed it.

"Hang on." The old man worked the gearshift, turning the pickup around. "I'm Amos Stiggims, by the way. I'm a farmer like my pappy before me and his pappy before him."

"I have an uncle who farms a little. He raises organic vegetables mostly."

"You don't say." Stiggims managed to grind through first and second gear as he chugged to the top of the rise. "I've never had much truck with those organic types. They look down their noses at me because I use what chemicals the law allows." He ground third, too. "They're like that uppity so-and-so on the television."

"Who?"

"You know. He's on late night. Always poking fun at folks like me. It's white trash this and white trash that. Somebody ought to shove a shotgun up his ass and pull the trigger." Stiggims cackled at the prospect.

Diana studied him without being obvious. He seemed harmless enough, just an old crank who hadn't come to terms with the outside world. But to be diplomatic, she sought to get on his good side by saying, "Topical humor doesn't do much for me, either."

Stiggims glanced at her sharply. "What kind of humor?"

"Topical. You know. About the news and the day's events."

Stiggims muttered something that sounded to Diana like "One of those."

"I beg your pardon?"

"Oh, nothing, girlie."

In the distance, well back from the road, sat a farmhouse, a barn, and outbuildings. Even that far off, Diana could tell they were like their owner and his truck: well past their prime. If she hadn't known better, she'd think they were built during the days of the Pony Express. Suddenly she sat up. "Mr. Stiggims, do you own a cell phone?"

"A what?"

"A cellular phone. I don't see any telephone lines to your property. Or maybe they bury the cable out here. Is that it?"

"Oh. The telephone. Sure, that's it. They bury the lines on account of the fierce thunderstorms and tornados we get. The winds are always knocking down trees and stuff."

A dirt track linked the road to the farmhouse. The pickup raised clouds of dust the whole length of it. As they braked,

Diana saw that she had given the buildings too much credit. Almost anywhere else, they would be condemned.

"Here we are. Come on in and make your call." Stiggims hopped out and started around the truck.

Diana had to jiggle the door handle a few times to get it to work. She climbed down and turned to get her backpack, saying, "I really appreciate this. The last thing I want is to be stranded. I need to get out of here as soon as possible."

"That's a pity," Amos Stiggims said.

"What is?"

It was then that Diana saw the tire iron.

Semper Fi

Seattle

As the man raised his rifle, Ben Thomas thrust his arm out the open window of his truck. The Double Eagle boomed and bucked twice, and the man, still wearing a lunatic grin on his lunatic face, melted to the asphalt. The hollow points made a mess of his head.

Ben looked at the dead drivers again. "Jesus," he said under his breath. He shouldn't be shocked, but he was. If his hitch in the Marines had taught him anything, it was to never put any cruelty past his fellow man. When he had been stationed in the Middle East, in the war that wasn't a war, he'd seen things that churned his gut and twisted his soul.

The other lesson Ben had learned was that there were no limits to hate. In the name of hatred all manner of atrocities were committed. Beheadings, mutilations, castrations, blowing children to bits and pieces. It had disgusted him. It had changed him. When he had gotten back, his wife kept saying he wasn't the same man. Hell, no, of course he wasn't. But how could he explain? What could he tell her that would help her see the horror? Words weren't enough.

So Ben had drifted deeper inside himself and they had drifted further apart, until one day he had come home and found a note saying that she couldn't take it anymore, couldn't take his dark silences, his lack of humor, and the cold front he put on. Little did she realize, it wasn't a front.

Now, placing his pistol on the seat, Ben chugged around the knot of vehicles. He would be damned if he were staying there until the cops showed up. They'd haul him in for questioning. Even if they eventually let him go, it could cost him days he couldn't spare.

There was barely enough room for Semper Fi to squeeze through the cars. He almost scraped her trailer on a building. Then he was past and he rumbled down the block to the next intersection.

Ben had a long way to go to get out of the city. He was down by the bay, near the aquarium and Waterfront Park. He needed to get to 90 east. Either he got on Interstate 5 and took 5 to where it merged with 90, or he stuck to the back streets. He figured the interstate would be jammed with people fleeing the city, so the back streets it was.

Not five blocks later he regretted his decision. Fourth Avenue was bumper to bumper and the overflow was spilling into the side arteries as everyone and their grandmother sought to bypass the jam. Since he didn't care to be boxed in, he wheeled into an alley and barreled down it. A Dumpster blocked his way, but Semper Fi knocked it aside with careless ease.

At the next street Ben turned. He wasn't sure which one he was on but he was heading in the right direction. Now and then he glimpsed the bridge.

Ben switched on the radio to the all-news station. The announcer was saying something about a nuclear strike on San

Diego. Ben only caught the tail end of the story. Then came an account of the Vatican going up in radioactive dust. China supposedly had declared war on the West.

Ben shook his head. He'd known it would come to something like this. The human race was *that* stupid. He wouldn't put it past homo sapiens to totally wipe themselves out.

A stop sign necessitated tromping on the brakes. Ben craned his neck to scan the next street—and his passenger door abruptly flung open. Instantly, Ben had a Double Eagle in his hand. He pointed it, but didn't shoot. "What the hell do you think you're doing?"

The girl looked to be all of sixteen. She wore scruffy clothes—scruffy by Ben's standards, but then he was old school—and had pink streaks in her black hair. She wore a nose ring and at least ten earrings in one ear. Her eyes weren't blue and they weren't green but some sort of in-between. "I need a lift."

"Not with me."

"Come on, mister. I don't own wheels, and I want out before it gets really bad."

"No. Slam the door on your way down."

"No, yourself." Incredibly, the girl climbed in. She shut the door and clasped her hands on her lap. "Ready when you are."

"The hell," Ben said. He didn't know whether to laugh or be mad. "Don't your ears work? Get your scrawny white ass out of my rig, and I mean now."

"You better get going or we'll get stuck here when it hits the fan." She smiled and held out a hand. "I'm Space, by the way."

"Space?" Ben repeated, despite himself.

"Yeah, I know. My real name is Geraldine, but I hate it. It's bogus. My great-grandmother or someone had it so my mom decided to honor her by giving me the name. Lame,

lame, lame. Anyway, when I was little, I was into stars and stuff. You know, astronomy. I liked it so much, my dad used to tease me and called me Spacey and somehow that got shortened to Space and here I am and here we are and you're wasting time."

"The hell," Ben said again.

"Are you catching flies? You really need to get your act together. If you want me out you'll have to throw me out, and I promise I'll scream and kick." Space reached out and tapped the Double Eagle. "And either use this or stop waving it in my face. You look silly."

To Ben's amazement, he lowered the pistol. "Listen, girl. I'm serious. I can't take you with me."

"Why not?" Space gazed about the cab. "It's not as if you don't have the room. Hell, this is the Ritz compared to some of the boxes I've slept in."

"Boxes?"

"Why do you repeat everything I say? Yeah, boxes. I live on the street a lot. And when you have no money and you don't want to sleep in the gutter, you find a box and crawl in. Boxes are everywhere. The big ones are comfortable enough, but the small ones are cramped. And some stink. And when it rains, well, a box ain't for shit, know what I mean?"

"Damn, girl."

"Can you *please* get this monster going? If a missile hits we'll be fried and I so don't want to go out as a piece of toast."

"Where are your parents?"

Space sighed in exasperation. "I just told you I live on the street. Do you think if I had parents they'd let me do that?"

"Everyone has parents," Ben persisted. "Either they're dead or you're a runaway or they threw you out because they couldn't take the motormouth."

Space had a nice grin. "Okay. You got me there. I run off

at the mouth a lot. But it's me, you know? I start talking and I can't stop. There are worse things. Like starting to drink and you can't stop. Or taking drugs and you can't stop. Not that I haven't never drank or never taken drugs, but I can stop both of them with no problem."

Ben set the pistol down, close to his leg. "I must be nuts."

"You're taking me, then?" Space beamed and clapped and bounced up and down. "Super. I wasn't sure if you'd be nice or if you'd be a perv. But I had to take the chance, you know."

Ben shifted into motion. He kept telling himself that if he had any sense he would throw her out. "Listen. I'll take you as far as the city limits. After that you're on your own."

"Where are you headed?"

"I'm on a run. I have a delivery to make in Minnesota."

"Isn't that a city somewhere?"

"It's a state. You're thinking of Minneapolis, which is a city *in* Minnesota. Right next to St. Paul. They call them the Twin Cities."

"Minnesota?" Space rolled it on her tongue as if tasting it. "Are the people there nice?"

"If you're thinking what I think you're thinking, you can forget it."

Space looked at him. "*You're* nice. You're trying to act all tough, but you're giving me a lift out of Seattle out of the goodness of your heart."

"Girl, I don't know why in hell I'm doing this." Ben was sincere. Ordinarily, he would open the door and give her a push. "I don't like people much."

"All people? Or just white folks?"

Ben and Semper Fi's gears growled at the same time. "Don't even try to lay that on me. I'm no bigot. I don't hate whites just because they're white. Although a lot of them hate me because I'm not." He came to another intersection and wheeled to the left. "When I say I don't like people, I mean *all* people. Black, white, red, yellow, polka-dot, you name it."

"That's harsh. You got a reason or is it you were born a grump and just got worse as you turned antique?"

"I'm thirty-four, girl. That's hardly antique."

"It's more than twice as old as me," Space said. Suddenly she pointed. "Look out!"

Ben had taken his eyes off the street. He glanced ahead, swore, and hit the brakes, hard. Another traffic jam took up most of the next block. A policeman was moving among the vehicles, gesturing and giving orders, apparently trying to get everything moving.

"Looks like we'll be stuck here for a while."

"Not if I can help it."

Another alley offered a way out. When the cop turned and started back the other way, Ben wasted no time in taking advantage of it. But he had barely nosed the truck in when he had to hit the brakes again. This time there wasn't just one Dumpster; there were five.

"God doesn't like you."

Ben didn't care if there were twenty. "God helps those who help themselves," he retorted, and gave her a demonstration of why Semper Fi was the next best thing to a bulldozer. All the Dumpsters were on wheels, so it was easy enough. The first pushed the second and they pushed the third, but the fourth spun and lodged against a wall. An extra tamp on the gas pedal, a loud crunch, and Semper Fi was out of the alley with Dumpsters rolling every which way.

A horn blared, and a compact car went flying past, the driver shaking a fist in fury.

"You made a friend there."

"Hush." Ben had traffic to contend with. He turned up

the radio, hoping for a traffic report. Instead, there was a bulletin; Israel had unleashed more nukes on her enemies.

"Just like in the Bible," Space said.

"Read it, have you?"

"Ouch. Is your middle name Sarcastic? That reminds me. What *is* your name?"

Ben told her.

"Well, you got it right. I hardly ever read, period. But I had grandparents. And Grandmom never went anywhere without her Good Book. She read parts to me every night when she tucked me in. And one of the books, I think that's what they call them, is about the stuff that's going down right now. About the end of the world."

"Not going to happen," Ben said, checking his rearview mirrors.

"What isn't?"

"What are we talking about? The end of the world, dope. It'll be bad, but the world will go on."

"Oh. I didn't know you were an expert."

"Two words, smartass. Hiroshima and Nagasaki."

"Who?"

"Don't you know anything? World War Two? The cities we bombed. With atom bombs?"

"Oh." Space nodded. "I've heard of them. I just didn't remember what they were called."

"I guess you didn't hear that fifty years after the bombs were dropped, both cities were fine. The people were healthy, the parks had flowers and trees, the water was safe to drink."

"So what are you saying? That we can bomb the hell out of the planet and fifty years from now things will be peachy?"

"Fifty. A hundred. I can't say how long it'll take." Ben shrugged. "Look at the past. Look at all the volcanoes, all the earthquakes, all the wars. You name it. The world will recover. The world always recovers."

"I wish I had your confidence."

Ben concentrated on driving. He wanted to get on the Greenway as close to where it crossed to Mercer Island as possible, on the theory that he'd have less congestion to deal with. To the best of his memory, that meant taking 167 and merging. He worried that he would find one or the other impassable, but for once things went smoothly.

Space pressed her nose to her window. "Is that Lake Washington down there?"

"What else would it be? The Pacific Ocean?"

"I only asked, smartass, because water makes me nervous. I can't swim." Space tore her gaze from the scenic splendor and shuddered. "I've always had this secret fear that one day I'll drown." She held up a hand. "I know. I know. But I can't help how I feel."

"You can breathe easy. I'm not about to drive through the guardrail. My truck can't swim, either."

"Funny."

Ben didn't let himself relax until they were past Lake Sammamish. By then they were rolling along at the speed limit. The traffic was heavy but not as bad as in the city.

"Don't we have mountains to go over?"

"There are a lot of mountains between here and Minnesota," Ben answered. They had seventeen hundred miles to cover, give or take, across some of the most rugged terrain on the continent. World War Three was raging across the globe and all sorts of lunacy and mayhem were breaking out from one end of the United States to the other.

"You have a strange look on your face," Space said. "What are you thinking about?"

"How much fun this is going to be."

Chaos Wind

New York City

The logjam of vehicles was worse at the exit. Two electric cars were wedged fast and had plugged the ramp for everyone else. Vehicles were stopped three across and ten deep. Many of the drivers were standing around talking or arguing.

"Not even this thing can get through that," Alf said.

Patrick Slayne didn't seem to hear him. He flicked a silver toggle switch and there was another loud *thunk*, this time from under the front end of the Hunster. The hood tilted upward a few degrees.

"What now?" Deepak wondered.

Slayne flicked another toggle switch and said quietly, "Vacate your vehicles. I repeat, vacate your vehicles."

To Deepak's surprise, the command was amplified fifty-fold. Everyone looked at the Hunster in puzzlement or wonder. Only a half dozen or so did as Slayne had instructed.

"Those who haven't done so, get out of your vehicles. In sixty seconds I am clearing the ramp."

"How will you do that without hurting them all?" Deepak inquired.

Slayne flicked off the toggle switch and said with the patient air of an adult explaining to a ten-year-old, "As you may have gathered by now, this vehicle is modified for special use. It's the gem in Tekco's fleet, the only one of its kind. But then, being the chief exec has its perks."

"Wait a minute. You're the *head* of Tekco Security? You run the whole company?"

"Run it. Founded it. Made it the premier global security firm," Slayne said with no small pride.

Alf exclaimed, "That's where I've seen you before! Your picture has been in magazines and on the news."

Slayne frowned. "It wasn't notoriety I sought. To be effective in my line of work I need to keep a low profile." His frown changed to a wry smile. "Listen to me. Talking as if the world will go on as usual." He shook his head, then flicked the same toggle switch and addressed the hidden microphone. "I'll give you ten extra seconds. This is your last warning."

Only a few drivers had complied. Several laughed or smirked as if it were some kind of joke. One man flipped his middle finger.

"There's our problem, right there," Patrick Slayne said to Deepak and Alf.

"What is?"

"Stupidity. It's been the downfall of the human race. Once the stupid ones outnumber the ones who give a damn, society disintegrates."

"What are you talking about?"

"Hold on tight," Slayne said, and placed the tip of his finger on a red button low on the dash. "There's quite a recoil."

"Quite a what?" Deepak wasn't sure he'd heard correctly.

Slayne turned the wheel so the Hunster was pointed at a wall to one side of the jam. He pressed the red button. The Hunster thundered and bucked and an explosion rocked the wall. Bits and chunks of concrete flew every which way, some as big as a basketball, most considerably smaller. People screamed. Those not in cars dived for cover.

A swirling cloud of dust enveloped everything.

Deepak peered into it, afraid of what he would see. Gradually the dust began to clear. He saw a few people bleeding but no bodies. Most of the vehicles caught in the hail of concrete had broken windshields and busted windows. "What have you done?"

"I'm getting you out of here." Slayne accelerated toward a huge hole in the wall. Or, rather, what was left of the wall next to the hole. "Brace yourselves. The battering ram can punch through concrete like it's paper, but there will still be a jolt."

There was. The sound was like the blast of a cannon. More of the wall shattered to bits, and through the gaping hole roared the Hunster.

Deepak looked back at the people who had been hurt by flying debris. "What's the matter with you? Don't you have a conscience? Do you realize what you've done?"

"I didn't kill anyone." Slayne turned up a ramp and the Hunster shoved a dust-caked hybrid out of the way with casual mechanical ease.

"Those were *people!* Living, breathing human beings. You hurt them. We should stop and help."

"No time. And if you don't mind some advice, you really should get hold of yourself."

Deepak tried to release the catch on his seat belt, but it wouldn't work. He tore at the belt. "Let me out. I've had enough. Tell Kurt Carpenter I no longer want to be part of his Endworld Protocol."

"The what?" Alf said.

"I'm afraid that's not possible," Slayne responded as he steered the Hunster around a compact.

"I've changed my mind, I tell you. I have that right. I wish the best for Mr. Carpenter, but I refuse to have anything to do with you."

"You're locked in."

"I'm what?"

"You stay that way until I decide otherwise."

"You're insane."

Patrick Slayne let out a sigh. "I'm one of the most rational people you'll ever meet, Mr. Kapur."

"It was wrong what you did."

"The only wrong is not to do the best you can at anything you put your mind to."

"You can't force me to go."

"Hold that thought." Slayne raced around a minivan and the Hunster burst from the bowels of a skyscraper onto East 52nd Street only half a dozen blocks from the East River. He turned right and braked sharply.

Ahead was a scene out of a disaster movie. Panicked people were running every which way. They didn't bother using crosswalks but darted in front of moving cars and trucks with no regard for their safety. Fortunately, traffic was moving at a crawl, partly due to congestion, and in part because more than a few drivers had abandoned their vehicles and joined the mad rush, their empty cars and trucks adding to the snarl.

Near the river a black column of smoke curled into the hazy sky. To the south was another, only the smoke was gray.

"Why don't I hear anything?" Alf asked.

Deepak had been wondering the same thing. Save for the muffled throb of the powerhouse under the hood, inside the Hunster they could hear themselves breathe.

"I killed the outside feed to spare our ears when I used the grenade launcher." Slayne flicked yet another toggle switch.

The interior blared with the discordant symphony of civilization in collapse. Shouts, curses, wails, screams, horns, and sirens assaulted the senses in a continuous barrage.

"How can it fall apart so fast?" Deepak marveled.

"Because the only thing holding it together was the fear of being arrested and thrown behind bars," Slayne said. "When all is said and done, the cop on the beat was the glue that held civilization together."

"That's so . . ." Deepak had to think to find the right word, ". . . cynical."

"It's realistic. Strip away those who enforce the laws we live by and those laws become so much hot air. Look around you. These people are looking out for number one. They don't give a damn about right and wrong." Slayne pressed the gas pedal and the Hunster growled into motion.

Deepak turned to Alf. "Can you believe this guy? He's like someone out of the Dark Ages."

"I agree with him."

"You're kidding. Alf, I've known you for, what, five years now? You've never once—"

Alf suddenly pointed and exclaimed excitedly, "Look!"

A young woman was fleeing along a sidewalk. In close pursuit came two men in scruffy clothes. She was almost abreast of an alley when she tripped and fell. The men were on her before she could rise. She fought them, kicking and shrieking, but they hauled her into the alley anyway.

"We've got to help her," Deepak urged.

"No."

"But they'll rape her, maybe even kill her. Are you telling me you can let that happen?"

Slayne scowled, and slammed on the brakes. He was out of the Hunster in a bound and ran to the alley.

Deepak saw Slayne draw his gun. He heard two swift cracks. Then Slayne came sprinting back and climbed in. "What did you do?"

"What did it look like?"

"You shot them?"

"I saved the woman. But you need to catch up with reality. You can't seem to get it through your head that my top priority is getting you of New York City in one piece. We can't afford any more distractions."

Deepak rarely cursed. His parents, both Hindus, deplored the habit, and he had never picked it up. But he cursed now, adding, "Damn it, Slayne. What manner of man are you?"

"The kind who does what he's told. Now quiet. I have some serious driving to do."

The streets were a chaotic nightmare. Stalled and abandoned vehicles, traffic backed up for blocks, pedestrians madly dashing to and fro, looters; New York City was bedlam unleashed.

Again and again Deepak tried to break free of the seat restraint and couldn't. Finally he resigned himself to the inevitable. Disgusted, he slumped back and glanced at Alf, who had been strangely quiet. "Are you all right? You haven't said anything for blocks."

Putting a finger to his lips, Alf whispered, "Shhhh. He's forgotten about me and I want to keep it that way. I'm safer in here with you than out there." Alf gestured at the madness running rampant.

Deepak had forgotten that Slayne had threatened to toss out his friend. He nodded in understanding and sought to keep Slayne distracted by saying, "Can you at least tell me how you intend to reach Carpenter's compound? I'm entitled to know that much, aren't I?"

Slayne patted the steering wheel. "You're sitting in it."

"In this? It could take weeks. What will you do for fuel? This behemoth can't get more than six miles to the gallon."

"Thirty-one. It's a hybrid. I intend to reach the compound in three days. No more, no less."

Deepak was skeptical. "You can't stay awake for seventy-two hours."

"That's why caffeine pills were invented. But I won't have to so long as we average forty miles an hour for twelve hours out of every twenty-four." Slayne wagged a finger at him. "Now for the last time, be a good little computer nerd and keep your mouth shut."

Simmering, Deepak lapsed into silence. He began to keenly regret ever agreeing to Kurt Carpenter's offer. At the time, it had seemed smart, what with world tensions being what they were. In hindsight he had shown great foresight. But he had never foreseen *this*.

Deepak expected his abductor, as he had begun to regard Patrick Slayne, to make for one of the tunnels or maybe even the George Washington Bridge, but instead he noticed they were winding toward the Hudson River, specifically, the piers in the vicinity of the heliport. He mentioned this fact out loud.

"I have to get you out of Manhattan. The bridges are all jammed. The tunnels, too. That leaves my contingency plan."

"Which is?"

"You'll see in a few minutes."

Deepak bunched his fists. The man could be exasperating. He contained his impatience and was soon rewarded with the surprising sight of a dilapidated warehouse at the water's edge. A structure so old, the sign was faded and blistered. He did make out an H and an L. "Surely not."

"The best place to hide something is in plain sight." Slayne stopped at a rusted gate that opened remarkably quietly when he slid a plastic card into a slot.

As he drove up to wide double doors, Slayne activated a switch. The doors rose on recessed rollers. Gloom enveloped them, then was relieved in a blaze of overhead florescent lights.

Alf pressed his nose to the glass. "I should pinch myself to be sure I'm awake."

The warehouse was immense. Unlike its exterior, the interior was a model of modernity. In contrast, mothballed in perfect condition, were old cars, old aircraft, and seacraft.

"Is this a museum?" Deepak asked.

"It belonged to one of the richest men of his day and age. A philanthropist, you might call him. A friend of a friend of an ancestor of mine." Slayne drove past a panel truck.

Alf grinned like a kid at a dinosaur exhibit. "I love this stuff. There's a submarine."

Slayne drove down the wide center aisle to what Deepak took to be a ferry afloat between thick pilings. On its bow was the name *Kull.* The gangway was down. Slayne drove up it and stopped on the foredeck. "Everyone out."

"Where's the crew?" Alf asked.

"You're looking at it."

Deepak wasn't asked to help, and he didn't. Slayne cast off the lines and climbed to the wheelhouse. Belowdecks the engine throbbed to life and the *Kull* edged toward a gigantic corrugated door. Just when Deepak was convinced they would smash into it, gears meshed, chains clanked and the door rose.

With superb finesse, Patrick Slayne steered the darkened ferry out into the Hudson.

Alf nudged Deepak. "Why isn't he using running lights?"

Before Deepak could answer, the night reverberated to the blare of a ship's horn and he looked up in horror to see a vessel bearing down on them.

Day of Wrath

Pennsylvania

Trudale was being looted. From his picture window on the second floor of his home, Soren Anderson saw men and women emerge from homes carrying laptops, stereo equipment and TV sets. One of the women carried a jewelry box under one arm and held a sparkling necklace.

"Why are they doing that?" Freya asked. "It's not right."

Magni raised wide eyes to his parents. "Will they come in here, Dad? Will they take all our stuff?"

Soren came to a quick decision. As yet, the looters were only at the turnoff into Wyndemere Circle. It would take them minutes yet to reach his place. Or so he hoped. "Grab your things and get in the truck. We're leaving."

"I haven't finished packing," Toril objected. "There's more I'd like to take. Especially if we're never coming back."

"What?" Freya said.

The looters approached the Simmons residence. Soren knew the family well; they often came over. George Simmons blocked his front door and tried to prevent the mob from entering. Simmons was pushed and shoved but refused to give way. Finally a burly man in grubby jeans and a T-shirt knocked Simmons down and others kicked and punched him senseless. Another moment and they were in his house. A scream wavered on the air.

"Odin protect us," Toril breathed. "Kids, do as your father says. Grab what you can and get to the truck." She dashed off with them in tow.

Soren ran down the stairs and out into the driveway. More screams and wails came from all quarters. A window burst with a tremendous crash. In the distance gunfire crackled. He considered going to the Simmonses' to see if he could help, but it would be folly to leave his own family unprotected. He turned to go back in.

Three human wolves were bounding along the hedge that bordered the next yard. In the lead was the same burly brute who had knocked down George Simmons. They came around the hedge, spotted Soren, and stopped.

"Nice truck you've got there, buddy," the burly one said.

"Leave."

The leader glanced at his companions, and the three spread out. One of them had a baseball bat. The third man flourished a folding knife with a six-inch blade.

Smiling smugly, the leader advanced and held out his hand. "Give us the keys and we'll let you be."

"No." Soren brought Mjolnir from behind his leg.

All three of them stopped.

"What the hell is that? A hammer?" The burly man laughed a hollow laugh that was echoed by his friends. "Mister, you give us any trouble, I swear to God I'll take that from you and beat your brains out."

"Go away." Soren held Mjolnir low in front of him and turned slightly so he could keep his eye on all three. The other two had started to circle. "I'm warning you."

A piercing shriek testified to the spreading savagery.

"You hear that?" the burly man said. "You got a family? You want that to happen to them? Hand over the damn keys and you can walk away."

Toril came running out, toting her suitcase. She stopped short and gasped. "Soren, what . . . ?"

"Stay where you are," Soren warned.

The three regarded her with glittering eyes. The burly one licked his lips and chuckled. "Well, now. This changes things. She's a looker, your woman. Might be I want a taste of that for myself."

Toril said angrily, "You're a pig."

"Look around you, lady. This ain't Disneyland no more. It's everyone for himself. We take what we want, when we want it, and I want you."

Soren had listened to enough. The insult to his wife made his blood boil.

He moved between them and Toril. "This is your last chance."

The burly man reached behind him and when his hand reappeared he held a butcher knife. "Cutting you will be fun."

Soren waited. His senses were incredibly acute: he could hear Toril's heavy breathing behind him; he could see beads of sweat on the burly man's brow; he saw the muscles on the arms of the man with the baseball bat tighten as the man prepared to attack.

They came in a rush. The bat arced at Soren's head. Sidestepping, Soren swung. Mjolnir and the baseball bat smashed together and the bat shattered and splintered.

The man with the pocketknife tried to stab Soren in the neck, but spinning, Soren caught him in the ribs.

Swearing luridly, the burly man darted in.

"Soren!" Toril cried.

Soren had seen him. Whirling, he swept his hammer up and around. The heavy steel head caught the man flush on his jaw. A loud crunch, an explosion of teeth and blood, and the burly man was down.

Soren swiveled to face the guy who'd had the baseball bat, but he was fleeing pell-mell down Wyndemere Circle. A warm hand touched his.

"Are you all right? Did they cut you?"

Soren could barely think for the throbbing in his temples. "No," he said thickly. "Get the kids. We've got to get out of here."

Toril nodded and took a step but looked back at him and smiled. "You were magnificent."

Blood dripped from Mjolnir. Soren wiped the hammer clean on the burly man's T-shirt and held it up to the sunlight so the metal gleamed brightly. "Sweet Asgard." He shook himself and held Mjolnir higher. "To the son of Odin I give thanks. Protect and deliver us from our enemies. A true son of Thor asks this in your name."

Smiling grimly, Soren scanned Wyndemere Circle to be sure none of the other looters were near, then hurried inside to help Toril. He felt strangely elated. Newfound vitality coursed through his veins.

Toril was shooing the kids ahead of her. Both had bulging backpacks and Magni was protesting, "But, Mom, I want my GamePro. And what about my skimboard?"

"Enough," Soren said sternly. "You will do as your mother says without argument. Is that understood?"

Magni was startled. "Sorry."

Freya had been gnawing on her lower lip. "Where are we going, Dad? Do you know somewhere safe?"

"Anywhere is safer than here." Soren hustled them to the pickup. He gave Magni and Freya a boost into the backseat.

A man holding a busted chair leg came running toward

them but stopped at the sight of the crumpled forms in the driveway.

Soren climbed in. Toril had her hands clasped on her knees, her knuckles white. He set Mjolnir between them and gunned the engine.

"What will happen to us, Soren? Will we be all right?"

Soren patted Mjolnir. "We'll be fine."

Nebraska

Professor Diana Trevor reacted without thinking. In the blink of an eye she had the mace up and out and had pressed the stud.

Amos Stiggims had started to raise the tire iron when the spray caught him full in the face. He staggered back, screeching. "My eyes are burning!" Blinking and coughing, he stumbled, fell to one knee, and let go of the tire iron. "You had no call to do that."

"You were about to hit me." Bending, Diana grabbed the tire iron and skipped out of his reach. "I was defending myself."

Stiggims couldn't stop shedding tears. Hiking his dirty shirt up around his scrawny chest, he daubed at his eyes. "Are you loco?" he demanded between swipes. "I was taking that inside is all."

"Sure you were. You need to change the tires on your couch. Is that how it goes?"

"Damn, you've got a suspicious nature. My freezer jams sometimes and that iron is how I pry it open."

Diana refused to take him at his word. "Why would you want to open your freezer?"

Stiggims stopped blinking long enough to glare. "I was thinking of inviting you to supper. But you can starve for all I care."

"I'd like to believe you. I really would." Diana was awash in a distinct sense of the absurd. "Here." She slid a hand under his arm and hoisted him to his feet. The skin-and-bones old goat was lighter than a feather.

Stiggims tore loose and moved toward the house. His face pressed to his shirt, he muttered under his breath.

Diana caught a few of his comments; they weren't flattering. Snatching her backpack, she ran ahead of him onto a dilapidated porch. "Here. Let me." She pulled on a screen door with more holes than screen.

"I don't want your help." Stiggims sulked. "Go back to the road and find someone else to pick on."

"I'm sorry." Diana followed him in and almost gagged. "What's that terrible smell?"

Stiggims stopped wiping and sniffed. "I don't smell anything but that stuff you sprayed me with. If I go blind it'll be your fault."

"You won't lose your sight," Diana assured him. She was so concerned about misjudging him that she hadn't paid much attention to her surroundings. Now she did, and she inwardly recoiled. The place was a pigsty. The floor was inches deep in trash and the walls were spattered with grime and food stains. "How can you live like this?"

"Like what? Alone? I don't cotton to people much."

Diana turned and something cracked under her foot. It was a chicken bone, partially chewed, the meat shriveled and moldy. Suddenly she needed out of there. She went onto the porch and gulped deep lungfuls of hot air. She was still holding the tire iron in one hand and her backpack and the mace in the other. Setting the pack down, she slid the mace into her pocket and went to lean the tire iron against the wall.

A growl brought her up short.

Out of the depths of the barn came a mongrel. A huge

dog, mostly black but speckled with white, it had the build of a St. Bernard. Blocky head hung low, it stalked toward her and bared its fangs.

"Mr. Stiggims!" Diana called. "Can you come out here, please? Your dog isn't happy to see me."

The old farmer didn't answer. Diana slowly backed to the screen door and opened it. "Mr. Stiggims?" The dog was still advancing so she backed inside.

Suddenly she felt a sharp pain in the small of her back.

"Drop that iron, dearie, and do it quick. If'n you don't, I'll cut you."

Diana glanced over her shoulder. Tears still streamed from Stiggims' eyes, but he had stopped blinking and was holding a knife to her spine. "What is this?"

The farmer jabbed harder. "I won't tell you again."

The dog was almost to the porch. It had stopped at the sound of Stiggims' voice but its hackles were up and it was snarling.

Diana let go of the tire iron and held her arms out from her sides. "There. Don't do anything hasty."

"I never do, girlie." Stiggims chuckled and came around in front of her. A spot of red was on the tip of the blade. "You had me worried for a bit. But now I can take you out to the barn." He jerked a thumb at the dog. "Hercules, there, will keep you company."

"Wait," Diana said, stalling. "Why are you doing this? What is it you want with me?"

"It's the end of the world, dearie. Armageddon. Just like in Scripture. Pretty soon the angels will sound their trumpets."

"But that doesn't explain what you want with *me.*"

"I want your company is all. A man shouldn't have to face the end times alone." Stiggims did a double take. "Oh. Was you thinking I had ideas? Dearie, I'm too old for such tomfoolery. We'll talk, and maybe play dominos, or cards if you like."

Diana thought he was insane.

Squaring his slim shoulders and drawing himself up to his full height, Stiggims solemnly declared, "'For the great day of His wrath has come, and who is able to stand?'"

"What was that? From the Bible?"

"You don't know the Good Book when you hear it? Of course it's from the Bible. Revelation 6:17 I know it front to back and back to front." Stiggims grew solemn again. "'And I looked, and behold, a pale horse. And the name of him who sat on it was Death, and Hell followed with him.'"

"Mr. Stiggims," Diana said, and caught herself. "Amos. Please. Listen to me. Holding me here against my will is illegal."

"There are none so blind," Stiggims said sadly.

Diana tried another tack. "It's not the end of the world. It's a war. World War Three. Millions will perish, but the world will go on. People will survive. You stand a good chance of living through it, living where you do."

"It's no use. I have my mind made up. I was sitting in that rocking chair thinking about how awful it was to go to perdition by my lonesome when you dropped out of the sky into my lap. I took that as a sign."

"Please. I have somewhere I need to be."

"You're darn right you do. My barn." Stiggims wagged the knife. "There's a small room in the back I use for tools and such. I can bar it, and there ain't any windows." He paused. "Or better yet, maybe I should put you in the root cellar."

"What about you? Where will you be?"

"I'll stay up here until the missiles start to fly. Then I'll join you."

"I'm sorry," Diana said. "That's unacceptable." She lunged, shoving him hard enough to spill him onto his backside on the porch. Whirling, she ran through the living room and into a small kitchen. The stench of rotten food assailed her as she raced to a back door and flung it open. Beyond was a yard and a cornfield, the stalks as tall as she was. Leaping down a short flight of steps, she sped toward them.

"Get her, boy! Attack! Attack!"

Diana looked back.

Hercules was after her.

Eve of Destruction

Washington

Ben Thomas's idea was to take Interstate 90 all the way across Washington and Idaho into Montana and then take Interstate 94 into northern Minnesota.

Things went fine as far as Spokane. They were able to get gas. He was careful not to let his fuel drop below half so he always had plenty to spare. Traffic wasn't the pain he expected it to be. A lot of folks were holed up in their homes, awaiting the next development in the spreading global conflict.

Space drove him nuts using the radio. She was constantly running up and down the dial looking for stations with the latest news. He almost told her to stop—but when she was playing with the radio she was usually preoccupied and quiet, and there was only so much of her chatter he could take. The girl about talked his head off.

It was as they were pulling out of Ellensburg that Space told Ben about her parents. Her father had been an alcoholic, her mother a druggie. When they hadn't been abusing each other, they had been abusing her. She had taken it until she was twelve and then she skipped. She had gone to live with an aunt who had always treated her nicely, but the aunt had a son her age who thought she was the hottest treat on two legs and couldn't keep his hands off her. So Space had skipped again and wound up living on the street.

"It wasn't bad at first. I had a little money so I could eat. I found a condemned building and lived in a room with a lock on the door so I could sleep safe at night. I stayed away from other street people. The few who knew I was hiding there left me alone. But the good vibes didn't last. They never do."

"Why didn't you go to the state for help? They could have found you a foster home."

"Would you want to live with people you didn't know? People who might have hang-ups of their own?" Space shook her head and her bangs swished. "No, I figured I was better off on my own. Even when the money ran out and I had to make do any way I could."

"You started turning tricks?"

Space cackled in glee and slapped her leg. "Only a man would think of that before anything else. I'm no skank. My body is mine, and making it with strangers isn't my idea of fun." She shook her head again. "I mainly stole to live. At first it was food. I'd go into a grocery store and stick stuff down my skirt."

Ben had been meaning to ask about her clothes. She wore all black, like one of those Goths. "What if the food fell out before you made it out the door?"

"I wore my skirt inside out so the pocket was on the inside. I'd slip whatever I stole into the pocket and waltz out with no one the wiser. But I could only take small stuff, and that was a drag. After a couple of hundred candy bars, the sweets aren't as sweet. Know what I mean?"

"I don't eat candy much."

"You will if there's nothing else you can get your hands on. I ate candy and I ate a lot of fruit. Bananas, mostly. It was easy to slip one into my pocket. I'm partial to pretzels, too. I'd open a bag and grab a handful. You wouldn't believe how easy it was."

"It's nothing to be proud of," Ben remarked. He wasn't a stickler for the law, but there were some things he would never do and stealing was one of them.

"Listen to you, Mr. Never Gone Hungry a Day in his Life. When your belly hurts from not eating, when you're so starved your skin is sticking to your ribs, you'll do whatever you have to. It's all about survival."

"I was a Marine, girl. And I'm black, besides. I know more about surviving than you'll ever learn."

"Oh, please. You had it rough because you weren't born white and you call that surviving?"

Ben flared with anger. He could have hit her, but he never hit females unless they were trying to do him harm. "Listen, you snot-nosed brat. What do you know about being black? About what it's like to be born into a world wearing skin that people hate because it's different from their own? To be sneered at? To be spit on? To be called the N word every time you turn around? That's how it was for me when I was little. But I didn't care. I gave it right back, and got stronger deep down, where it counts. Strong enough to be a Marine. To be one of the few, the proud. And to be so damn tough, no mother's son better mess with me or he'll eat his goddamn teeth."

"Touched a nerve, huh?"

Ben swore. The race issue always set him off.

"Hey, it's cool. You don't take crap from anybody. I admire that. All I'm saying is that you survived in your way and I survived in mine, and for you to look down your nose at me because I did it different isn't fair."

Ben thought about it and grudgingly replied, "You have a point. No insult meant."

"None taken." Space grinned. "Just think. Two badass survivors like us, this end-of-the-world deal should be a breeze."

The radio was nothing but war talk. Even the stations that usually played music were doing news, and none of it was good. The war in the Middle East had spread. Russia and China were involved. Israel was fighting for its life. North Korea was marshalling troops along its border with South Korea. A South American dictator had invaded his neighbor.

On the national front, the president appealed for calm. Looting and random violence were everywhere. Martial law would be imposed as soon as the National Guard was fully mobilized.

"What will you do if they close the highways?" Space asked.

Ben hadn't thought of that. But it didn't matter. "When I give my word to make a delivery, I keep it."

They made it out of Washington. Ben refueled at Coeur d'Alene and pushed on into the Bitterroot Mountains. Exits were fewer and farther between. Hardly any other vehicles were on the road. There was talk on the radio that Chinese subs had been spotted off the West Coast, that a Russian fleet was bound for the East Coast. Terrorist activity was on the rise. There was worry a U.S. city would be nuked. On and on went the litany of fear.

The Bitterroots were so remote that Ben didn't anticipate trouble. So long as the gas stations stayed open, he would be all right. But he wasn't a machine. He'd kept himself awake with caffeine pills, but he needed sleep and he couldn't put it off any longer. He told Space.

"Fine by me. Get a room with cable. I love movies."

"Sorry, girl, but I'm not stopping at a motel. I bunk in my cab."

"Spoilsport."

The next exit was a small town called Smelterville. Ben had never been there. He slowed to a crawl and braked at a stop sign. A gas station had a CLOSED sign in the window, but that was all right; the truck had nearly three-quarters of a tank. He wheeled on into Smelterville. The streets were deserted. There wasn't a soul in sight.

"This is spooky."

Ben was looking for a place to pull over. A sign announced a park. He turned down a side street, the diesel rumbling, and came to a stop next to a grassy knoll speckled by trees and picnic benches. "This will do." He pulled to the curb and turned off the ignition.

In the sudden silence the quiet around them seemed unnatural. The park was empty of life. Not so much as a bird or a squirrel anywhere. Across the street were a few frame houses and a mobile home, as still as tombstones.

"Where is everyone?" Space nervously asked.

"Trembling in their boots." Ben pocketed the keys. "I'm climbing in the back for a few hours. You stay put until I wake up. I don't want you wandering off, you hear?"

Space grinned and gave him a sharp salute. "Sir, yes sir."

"Goof." Ben parted the curtain and climbed into the bunk. He curled on his side and closed his eyes. As he was drifting off, he thought he heard the rasp of a door handle. Then sleep claimed him.

New York

Deepak Kapur's heart leaped into his throat. He thought for sure he was going to die. The ship bearing down on the *Kull* was so close that he swore he could see rivets on its hull, which was preposterous, given that it was night and that except for the ship's deck lights high above, it was so dark it was a wonder those onboard had spotted the ferry. Then it hit him. They *didn't* know the *Kull* was there. They were blowing the horn for some other reason. A collision was inevitable.

He took a step back and braced for the impact, fully expecting to be crushed to pulp. Suddenly the ferry gave a lurch that nearly unbalanced him and the deck tilted at the bow. A high-pitched roaring whine came from under his feet. The next instant the ferry shot forward as if jet propelled.

Alf bleated in terror.

The ship was almost on top of them. White lettering identified it as the *Coral Sea*. Her bow passed so close to the ferry's stern that Deepak could have reached out and touched it. Then they were in the clear and heading downriver. Collecting his wits, he climbed to the wheelhouse and went in without knocking.

Patrick Slayne was at the helm consulting a digital display. He didn't look up. "What do you want? I'm busy."

"You almost got us killed."

"I knew the ship was there. I had it on radar. Once I activated the hydrofoil it couldn't touch us."

"Hydrofoil?" Deepak was making it a habit of repeating things the man said.

"Didn't you feel the deck move?" Slayne looked up from the display. "Ever hear the expression, 'the bigger the boy, the bigger his toys'? As the CEO of Tekco, my toys are the wares my company uses and sells. The Hunster, this hydro, and more you couldn't imagine. I'm the ultimate tech geek."

Somehow Deepak couldn't imagine him as a geek of any kind. "What do you plan to pull out of your high-tech grab bag that will get us to Minnesota safe and sound?"

"I'm saving it for a surprise. But first things first." Slayne consulted the display. "I'm going to bring us in just above the Narrows. From there we'll cut across to 78."

"I hope you know what you're doing."

"I always do." Slayne turned the wheel while watching the display. "You should give me more credit. But then, Kurt Carpenter did say your psych profile showed you have a superiority complex."

"What?"

"You tend to think you're better than everyone else. Sorry, that's not entirely true. You tend to think that you're *smarter* than everyone else. I suppose there's a difference, but to me it's all the same."

"Carpenter let you study my psych profile?" Deepak had understood that all personal information was to be held in the strictest confidence.

"I'm one of the inner circle, Mr. Kapur. I designed the bunkers. I designed a special vehicle you know nothing about. I stocked the armory. In short, anything and everything having to do with security is under my oversight."

"That's no excuse for Carpenter letting you see my psych tests."

"Ah. But it is. Kurt needs you. The people at the compound need you. You're a genius with computer systems, and we'll need to rely on our computers heavily for the first ten years or so."

"Ten years?"

"Projections, analysis, communications, those sorts of things. Don't worry. The bunkers are shielded. We should be EMP-proof. I say should because the shielding hasn't been tested under actual combat conditions. We couldn't hardly set off a nuke, now, could we?"

"But ten *years?*"

"Maybe longer if the solar arrays and the batteries hold out. No one knows how widespread the aftereffects will be, or even what they'll be. Oh, radiation is a given. But there are a host of biological and chemical weapons out there, and only a computer can even begin to make sense of the permutations."

Deepak began to realize that this man was more than muscle with a gun. "So that's why Carpenter thinks I'm essential."

"You *are*, Mr. Kapur. The sooner that sinks in, the better we'll get along. Now why don't you join your friend? I'll be busy for the next ten minutes or so."

Alf was at the rail, his face pale in the starlight. "Listen to that, will you? We're lucky to be out of it."

From both shores rose the sounds of sirens and wails and occasional screams. Flashing emergency lights pierced the dark. They passed a well-lit pier where people were fighting over small craft.

"If it's this bad now," Alf said, "what will it be like when the missiles hit?"

He answered his own question. "It'll be insane. Only the strong will make it, and me, I never was very strong."

"Just remember you're not alone. I'll be at your side, come what may."

"Thanks, pal."

The *Kull* swung in parallel with the shore and bore to the south, still without running lights. Eventually it slowed and the deck dipped until it was level. Ahead was a dock bathed by a single light. Beyond that was a brick building.

"There's no one around," Alf observed. "It looks safe enough."

The *Kull* eased broadside to the dock. Out of the wheelhouse bounded Patrick Slayne. With great urgency he saw to the gangway, then ran to the Hunster and beckoned. "What are you waiting for? Get in."

Deepak and Alf went over but they were in no particular hurry until Deepak asked, "What's the rush?"

"I've been monitoring government frequencies. Homeland Security just got the word. We don't have much time."

"Time for what? Are the highways such a mess we'll never make it out?" Alf asked.

"It's not that." Slayne gazed skyward. "New York City is about to be nuked."

Fractured Lives

Pennsylvania

It got worse the farther west they went.

The National Guard had been called in to quell the panic and the looting, but most soldiers were sent into the bigger towns and cities. Rural America was left largely on its own.

It was only a hundred miles or so from Trudale to Harrisburg, but it might as well have been a thousand. The interstate was a mess. Twice, early on, Soren had tried taking 76, and each time, within a dozen miles, he had come upon tangles of vehicles. The secondary roads were mostly clear, but they took a lot longer.

Toril wouldn't stop fretting. "What if something has happened to her? What if a mob ransacked her house like they did our neighbors?"

"I very much doubt it," Soren sought to soothe her. "Your mom lives in the country. She should be fine."

"It's near Interstate eighty-one," Toril reminded him.

"Half a mile, at least." Soren couldn't see anyone tramping that far just to loot an old farmhouse.

Freya and Magni were strangely quiet. Normally they bickered and teased but now they sat staring fearfully out the windows.

Soren had tried to get them to play "I see . . ." where one tried to guess what the other was looking at. He had tried to get them to play the license plate game, where they got points for each out-of-state license. He had tried to get them to sing. They declined and went on staring.

The radio started acting up. Now and then static and strange sounds drowned out the announcers. Soren wanted the latest news and kept switching stations. Late in the afternoon he stumbled on a pair of bombshells.

> *". . . It is officially confirmed that San Diego has suffered a nuclear strike. It has also been confirmed that the Vatican has been destroyed. Initial reports indicate a backpack nuke was used. In the Mideast, Israel has launched multiple air strikes. Tehran has been hit hard, and there is word that much of that city is radioactive waste. From the U.S. Navy comes word of a fleet of warships bound for the eastern coast of the United States. It's believed that New York and Philadelphia . . ."*

Static cut in. Soren tweaked the dial, but it did no good. He had lost the signal.

They swung east of Harrisburg. Their route took them near Indian Echo Cave, which Soren had visited as a boy, and on through Hummelstown to within a mile of 81. A turnoff took them along a country road past several farms.

At last the familiar white stucco farmhouse atop a hill came into sight.

Toril sat forward and clasped her hands. "If only we could have gotten through to her. She could be ready to go."

"We'll spend the night," Soren offered. The sun was already perched on the horizon, and a night's sleep in comfortable surroundings would do the children good.

Gravel crunched under their tires as Soren wound up a long drive flanked by stately maple trees. He braked next to a lilac bush and everyone piled out. He brought Mjolnir with him.

The rocking chair on the porch was empty, the house quiet. Toril dashed up the walk and knocked eagerly. When there was no reply, she tried the doorknob. "It's locked."

"Maybe Sigrid is watching television and didn't hear you."

"Or she doesn't have her hearing aid in." Toril went to a potted plant, lifted it, and produced the key.

The house always smelled of food. Today Soren would swear it was oatmeal. He followed his wife into the living room, but Sigrid wasn't there. A dark hall led past the dining room, with its mahogany table and chairs, and into the kitchen.

"Where can she be? She wouldn't go anywhere at a time like this." Suddenly stopping short, Toril raised a hand to her throat. "Mother!"

Sigrid Uhlgren sat slumped over the kitchen table, one arm under her head, the other dangling.

Toril ran over and grabbed her by the shoulders. "Mother? What's wrong? Speak to me!"

Soren confirmed that Sigrid would never speak again. She wore a peaceful expression, as if dying had been a pleasant passage from here to the hereafter. He looked at his wife and shook his head.

"But *how?*" Toril cried. Bending over her mother, she began to sob.

Soren suspected a heart attack or stroke. Sigrid had been in her late seventies and in failing health ever since her husband had died. She simply hadn't cared to live without her Karl.

"Mom?"

Soren quickly ushered the kids to the living room and told them to stay put. Then he went out to the truck. He still intended to stay the night, and they would need their backpacks.

When he returned, Toril had stopped crying, but her cheeks and chin were wet. Sniffling, she tenderly stroked Sigrid's hair. "I loved her so much. She was as good a mother as anyone could ask for."

Soren agreed. Sigrid had accepted him dating her daughter long before Karl had. Maybe her intuition had told her he was the one. Or maybe it was that they were so much alike. She had been steeped in the old ways, and while she hadn't believed as he did, she'd respected his right to do so. "Do we burn her according to the old ways or bury her? She's your mother, so the decision should be yours."

"What if someone saw the smoke and came to investigate? Burying is fine."

Soren doubted anyone would come, but they were pressed for time. "Okay."

"Give me a few minutes. I want to pay my respects."

Soren went out and over to the garden shed. Inside was the shovel he needed. Where to dig was the next question. He chose a spot near the rose bushes. Roses had been Sigrid's passion.

Toril insisted on a service. She brought the children outside and they stood around the fresh mound of earth with their heads bowed.

" 'I know where stands a hall brighter than sunlight,' " Soren quoted. " 'Gleaming better than gold in Lee-of-flame.

Hosts of the righteous shall inherit it, and live in the light everlasting.' "

Supper was a sorry affair. Toril made soup, but only Soren was hungry. The kids asked to be excused. Toril put down her spoon, leaned her elbows on the table, and placed her face in her hands.

"I'm sorry. I'm too broken up."

"She was your *moder*," Soren said quietly. "The healing will take time."

"Thank you for saying the words. I couldn't think."

Soren reached across and gently placed his hand on her arm. "Don't be so hard on yourself." He couldn't help wondering, though, if maybe a different passage would have been more appropriate. One, in particular, had stuck in his mind most of the day. *The sun will go black and the earth sink into the sea. Heaven will be stripped of its bright stars. Smoke will rage, and fire, leaping living flame, will lick heaven itself.*

Toril looked up and said, "My father had a gun."

"What?"

"A shotgun. In the closet in their bedroom. He didn't shoot it much, but it should still be there."

Soren glanced at Mjolnir on the table beside them. "I'll rely on my hammer."

"What if we run into looters with guns? You're not Thor. You can't call down the lightning and the thunder."

"Would that I could." Everyone had a secret yearning they rarely revealed, and Soren's was that he would dearly love to be the true and real God of Thunder. Childish, but there it was.

"What will happen to us? What will happen to our children?" Toril gazed out the window at the gathering darkness. "What will the world be like when this madness is over?"

Soren didn't say anything but he was thinking, Maybe it never will be over.

Professor Diana Trevor had no hope of getting to the cornfield before Hercules caught her. She veered toward the barn and ducked around its wide door, pressing her back to the wall. She heard the dog's heaving breathing and the pad of its paws, and the next second it hurtled past her and slid to a stop in the dusty barn. She held her breath, afraid the sound of her own breathing would give her away, as Hercules stalked toward the rear. He didn't think to look behind him.

Diana needed something to defend herself with. Her eyes took a few more moments to adjust, and then she could see the straw that littered the floor and a ladder leading to the hayloft. Propped against the ladder was a pitchfork.

Diana would be damned if she were going to let the old farmer throw her into his root cellar. She had somewhere to be, and she would get there no matter what it took.

Boots pounded, and Amos Stiggims entered. He was still holding his folding knife. He ran a dozen steps farther, then stopped. "Where is she, boy? Where did that tricky bitch get to?"

Diana gauged the distance to the ladder. It would put her near Stiggims, but it couldn't be helped. The mongrel was halfway to the rear of the barn and posed no immediate threat.

"Find her, boy," Stiggims urged. "I saw her come in. She has to be here somewhere."

Girding herself, Diana bounded toward the ladder. She was almost to it when both Stiggims and the dog heard her. Hercules spun and growled. Amos bleated an oath and lunged, trying to grab her.

Diana barely skipped aside in time. Another long stride and she had the pitchfork, then she turned to confront them. Amos stopped cold, a twisted smile on his face. Hercules stopped, too, but only for a few heartbeats. Then he slunk forward.

"Stay, boy! Stay!" Siggims commanded. To Diana he said, "Be reasonable. Put that down. I don't want to hurt you. All I want is your company."

"For how long?" Diana shot back. "A year? Five years? A lifetime? No thank you."

"It won't be so bad. I'll treat you decent. I'll keep you fed and let you take baths and everything."

"You're all heart."

The farmer stiffened in indignation. "No need to take that tone. You could be worse off. You could be on the road with no one to look after you."

"I don't need babysitting. I'm a grown woman." Diana was keeping an eye on Hercules. He was still in a crouch and could spring in a twinkling.

"All the more reason for you and me to stick together, girlie. Like I told you, I don't intend no frisky business."

Hercules took another step and Diana turned, the pitchfork in front of her. "Warn him off or so help me I'll stick him."

"Stay, damn it!" Stiggims spread his arms in appeal. "Let's talk this out, you and me. We can work things out so they benefit both of us."

"You're crazy, old man," Diana said flatly. "I don't care if it is the end of the world. You can't do as you please with every female who comes along."

"There's only been you. It won't be so bad. I have plenty of food stored. The rest of the world will starve, but we'll have full bellies."

Diana had to get out of there. The dog was inching toward her. Then Amos moved so he was between her and the door. "Out of my way. I'm leaving."

"I'm more spry than I look, girlie. And Hercules, there, is a regular lion when he's mad. Make it easy on yourself. Drop that thing and come along without a fuss."

"Please, Mr. Stiggims. I don't want to hurt you."

"That's damn decent of you. It truly is. But you're putting the cart before the horse."

"Please."

"Beg all you want. I've made up my mind." Stiggims crouched and showed his yellow teeth.

"There are limits and I have reached mine."

"Is that so? Then it's root hog or die, girlie."

"Call me that one more time."

"What? Girlie?" Stiggims chuckled. "Gets your dander up, does it?"

Diana clenched the pitchfork harder.

"Are you one of those feminazis I hear about on the radio?"

"No, I'm a pissed-off *woman.*" Diana lunged, but it was only a feint. She expected him to do what he did, namely, spring back and bawl at the dog.

"Get her, Hercules! Attack, boy!"

Whirling, Diana braced the long handle against her side, the pitchfork angled up. The dog was already in midair. It came down right on the tines, yipping as they ripped through its body like knives through butter. The dog weighed as much if not more than she did, and she was knocked back.

"Hercules!" Amos Stiggims cried. He stared at the dead dog, then screeched and came at her like one possessed.

Letting go of the pitchfork, Diana evaded a wild slash. She backpedaled and Stiggims came after her, his eyes lit with maniacal fury. He swung the blade at her throat, her chest, her face. She bumped into something and nearly fell. Reaching back to steady herself, she realized she had collided with the ladder. Darting around it, she tried one last time.

"It doesn't have to be like this." She tried to stay calm. "Drop the knife and let me leave."

"*Bitch!*" the old man shrilled, and thrust his knife between the rungs.

Diana had her bi-weekly volleyball sessions to thank for the reflexes that enabled her to grab his wrist, wrench with all her might, and break the bone with an audible *crack*. He screamed and slumped, and she came around the ladder and landed an uppercut any boxer would envy. It nearly broke her hand, but it left him on his knees, too woozy to resist as she dived a hand into his pocket and palmed the keys.

Five minutes later the truck was roaring down the country road, raising a thick cloud of dust in its wake.

Diana Trevor gripped the wheel tightly. She had a long way to go and nothing was going to stand in her way.

Except dying.

The Color of God

New York City

Patrick Slayne drove with fierce intensity. He needed to put as much distance behind them as he could in as short a time as possible. He pushed the Hunster past ninety when the streets permitted and took curves perilously fast.

Alf Richardson was as pale as snow. "It's like being on a roller coaster, only worse."

"Can't you slow down?" Deepak Kapur complained.

"Of course I can," Slayne responded. "But I won't. Unlike you, I happen to like breathing."

Deepak made a prediction of his own. "You'll want to kick yourself for being ridiculous when nothing happens."

"You're in denial, Mr. Kapur."

"Or is it that I have more confidence in the U.S. military than you do? They have satellites that can shoot missiles down. They have land-based defense systems like the Nimrod that was set up last year. They have jet interceptors."

"Your point?"

"This isn't Iran. This isn't Israel. It's America. We have the most sophisticated weaponry on the planet. I doubt very much that an enemy missile will get through."

"That's because you're under the delusion that our defenses are infallible. Trust me. They're not. Satellites work best against missiles with high trajectories. They don't do as well against missiles that fly at ground or sea level. The Nimrod is effective, yes, but again, it's hard for the system to lock in on a missile that comes in low. As for our jets, by the time they're scrambled to intercept, it will be over."

"I refuse to believe that."

"Like I said, you're in denial."

Alf cleared his throat. "I believe you, Mr. Slayne. You've been right about everything else."

Slayne didn't appear to hear him. "Our lives depend on the payload. I'm guessing it will be one kiloton, but it could be more."

"How far do we have to go be to be safe?" Alf asked.

"Completely safe? Thirty miles."

"How far have we come?"

"We're not quite six miles outside the city."

Alf clutched his seat. "Oh, God."

"Stay calm, Mr. Richardson. The Hunster is shielded and reinforced. Essentially, it's a disguised tank. Or a Humvee, if you want. We can handle ten times the radiation of most any transport on the planet." Slayne spun the wheel, taking a corner on two tires. "Our main worry is the blast pressure. Up to five miles out from ground zero, the pressure wave can flatten a building."

Deepak interjected, "Did you ever stop to think that Homeland Security might be wrong?"

"Think what you will if it will make you happy."

Sighing in annoyance, Deepak shifted in his seat and looked out the rear window at the New York skyline. It looked so serene; the skyscrapers were silhouetted against the sky in grand majesty. Suddenly there was a flash brighter than the sun, a flash so brilliant, Deepak cried out and looked away. When he glanced back through slitted eyes he beheld a purple glow. His eyes began to hurt and he looked away once more, but only for a few seconds.

A mushroom cloud was taking shape. So was a wall of living flames that leapt outward from the impact point, consuming everything in its path.

Alf screamed and doubled over. "I'm going to be sick!"

"You do and I throw you out," Slayne snapped.

Deepak barely heard them. He was riveted to the most awe-inspiring sight of his life. The purple had changed to red. The mushroom cloud was at ten thousand feet and rising. On an impulse he timed it with his wristwatch. In less than a minute the cloud was thirty thousand feet high. The stalk stretched as the cloud rose.

"Magnificent," Deepak exclaimed.

"You can't mean that," Alf bleated in terror.

Deepak could almost see the shock waves rippling outward like ripples in a pond. Whatever they touched, they flattened or blew apart. With remarkable speed the waves swept toward them.

"Faster!" Alf urged.

Slayne pushed the Hunster to a hundred. "Hold on tight. We'll be like bugs in a barrel."

Deepak wondered what that meant. Then there was no time for wondering; the shock waves caught up with them. The Hunster gave a hard lurch and spun completely around. Clutching the handle over the door, he pressed his feet against the floor.

"Oh, God," Alf wailed. "We're dead!"

"Here comes the worst of it!"

Pressure waves buffeted the Hunster. Slayne tried to

maintain control, but human sinews were no match for potent, raw, incalculable force. The Hunster went into a tailspin, and then went on spinning. A building loomed in the windshield, growing closer and closer.

Deepak had barely braced himself when the Hunster slammed into a wall hard enough to make his ears ring. He slumped in his seat, half dazed, then groped about his body checking for broken bones.

Alf was groaning.

At the base of the mushroom cloud was a purple dome, a gigantic pulsing, swelling, gelatinous bubble. It spread outward from the epicenter until it had swallowed half a mile of city. It appeared to be yards thick and almost looked wet.

A shiver ran down Deepak's spine. "I have seen the face of Shiva, the Destroyer." He would never be the same.

"Get us out of here!" Alf urged.

Slayne was trying. He turned the ignition, but all the engine did was growl. He tried again, and a third time, then smacked the dash. "This shouldn't happen. We're shielded."

Deepak looked back at the purple bubble, which was pulsing and writhing with nuclear life.

"What *is* that thing?"

A roar from the engine brought a yip from Slayne. He threw the Hunster into gear to get clear of the wall, then wheeled to the west and tramped on the gas pedal. "Hang on. We need to vacate the radiation zone as quickly as possible."

"What happens if we don't?"

"We die of radiation poisoning, Mr. Richardson. As grisly a death as you can conceive."

Deepak didn't care about that. He didn't care that Slayne was driving like a lunatic. He couldn't take his eyes off Shiva, made real. Belatedly, he realized that the majestic skyscrapers he had been looking at only minutes ago were gone. So were countless other buildings and homes. A great circular swath of steel, stone, and humankind had been consumed, the very heart of New York City devoured by the ultimate man-made monster.

"Will we make it, Mr. Slayne?" Alf asked.

"Time will tell."

Idaho

The pain brought Ben Thomas back to life. He started to groan and bit it off. Opening his eyes, he gazed around himself in confusion. He thought it must be night; it was so dark. Gradually his eyes adjusted. He was in a room. There was the outline of a door on one wall, but no windows. He went to move and discovered his wrists and ankles were tied.

"Damn me for a fool."

From a patch of ink in a corner came a squeal of delight. "You're alive! That knock on the head didn't kill you."

"Space?" Ben's tongue felt inches thick. He blinked and realized something was wrong with his left eye.

"Who else?" She wriggled out of the dark, her arms and legs tied as his were. "I'm sorry they got you, too. It's my fault."

Ben remembered now. He had woken up in the truck and found her gone so he had gone looking for her. He'd called her name over and over and when she didn't answer he had gone from door to door. No one answered his knocks. He was starting to think Smelterville was deserted when he came to an old factory. He'd almost passed it by, but he had glimpsed movement at a window and went to investigate. He had knocked and tried the door. It was unlocked so he had poked his head in—and that was the last he remembered until now. "How long have I been out?"

"A couple of hours. They dumped us here and said they'd be back later."

Ben tested the rope around his wrists. There was slack but not much. He set to work moving his forearms back and forth. "Who's this 'they' you keep talking about?"

"I don't know. They didn't say a whole lot." Space continued to wriggle toward him.

"How did they catch you?"

"I was exploring. I know you told me to stay in the cab, but I was bored." Space frowned. "I didn't think it would hurt if I took a look around."

"Now you know better." Ben gritted his teeth against the pain he was causing himself.

"I couldn't find anyone. Then I saw a grocery store, a mom-and-pop deal, and figured I'd buy a Three Musketeers. I love Three Musketeers. They're my favorite candy in all the world. I could eat a whole box at one sitting. I'd be in heaven."

"Space, damn it."

"What?"

"Forget the stupid candy and tell me how they caught you."

"Geez. You're a real bear when you get a knock on the head." Space was almost to him. "But it was like this, see. I went into the store and there was no one behind the counter, so I helped myself. I was coming back out when half a dozen of them closed in. I ran, but they know the town better than I do and I got trapped in an alley with no way out."

"What can you tell me about them? Anything at all will help." The Marines—and Ben—were big believers in "know your enemy."

Space stopped. "They're guys with guns. A whole lot of guys. One of them said I was an outsider and from now on outsiders don't get to come and go as they please."

Ben wondered if he could bribe them. He had a roll of bills hidden in Semper Fi.

"A young one whispered to me that he was sorry about what they were doing, but there was nothing he could do."

"Did he tell you his name?"

"Roger."

Ben filed the information for future reference. It might come in handy; it might not. The important thing was that at least one of their captors had a conscience.

"What do we do? Do you have a plan to get us out of here?"

"As a matter of fact, I do."

"What is it?" Space eagerly asked.

"We get in my truck and ride like hell." Ben tried twisting his right wrist and paid for it with a spike of a pain.

"You're not taking this serious."

"I always take dying serious." Ben felt wet drops trickle down his wrist, but he kept at it. There was no telling when their captors would return.

No sooner did the thought cross his mind than feet tramped toward them and the door was pulled open. A hand reached in and found a switch. Light from an overhead bulb flooded the room and in filed four men. They wore everyday clothes. One had on a Mariners baseball cap; he couldn't have been more than twenty and he had more freckles than a beach had sand. He came and stood over Ben. "Good. You're awake."

"Who do you think you are, treating us like this? Let us go or I'll report you to the law."

The young man laughed. "Do you hear him, boys? This here darkie is threatening us."

"What did you just call me?"

"Listen up, darkie. My name is Hardin. I'm one of Myron Croft's lieutenants. We're setting up a new order with laws of our own." Hardin drew back his leg. "This is what I think of you and your kind."

Ben tried to roll out of the way, but he was much too slow. A steel-toed boot caught him in the ribs. Sheer agony coursed through him, but he refused to give them the satisfaction of seeing him in torment. Holding his head high, he put on his best poker face and said, "Is that all you've got, punk?"

Hardin grinned. "We've got us a tough mother. Good. You'll last longer. We'll have us more fun."

"Leave him be," Space said angrily. "We never did anything to you, you little twerp."

Hardin had ignored her, but now he turned and bent low so his face was above hers. "The slut speaks."

"Slut, am I?" Space tried to butt him with her forehead.

"Dressed the way you are, what else would you be but one of those city girls who gives it out for free?" Hardin nudged her with his boot. "But you'll learn. You and your black friend, both."

"Why are you doing this?"

"Haven't you guessed? It's the end of the world, girl. We just heard that New York City has been nuked. San Diego and maybe Seattle, too."

"What does that have to do with us?"

"You sure are dumb. Pretty soon there won't be any government. It'll be every dog for itself. Now Myron, he's real smart. He saw this would happen and he got us set for it." Hardin puffed out his chest. "We're taking over, lock, stock, and barrel."

Space sneered in contempt. "You take over one little town and act like you're God?"

"Not one town, stupid. We're taking over all of Idaho. First this part and then the rest." Hardin turned back to Ben. "Now then. Suppose you tell us what's in that trailer you're hauling."

"None of your business."

"That's where you're wrong, mister. Anything we want, we take. We tried to break the lock but it's made of some newfangled metal. So I'll ask you again and if you don't answer me, we'll see if you're as tough as that lock." He tapped his foot. "Well? I ain't got all day."

Fully aware of the consequences, Ben Thomas squared his shoulders and said in fierce delight, "Go to hell."

The Eye of The Storm

Minnesota

Kurt Carpenter was at his desk in C Block when there was a rap on the door and Becca Levy poked her head in.

"They're here."

"Send them in." Carpenter rose to greet the three men. "I'm glad you made it."

Patrick Slayne had a three-day growth on his chin, and his suit had the rumpled look of clothes that had been slept in. "Kurt," he said warmly as they clasped hands. "It's good to see you again."

"How bad was it out there?"

Slayne claimed an easy chair and crossed one leg over the other. "The worst was New York City. We barely made it out."

"Yes. Becca relayed your message. You actually saw the missile hit?"

"Mr. Kapur and his friend saw more than I did. I was too busy driving."

Carpenter turned to Deepak Kapur. "Thank God you're alive. I consider you essential to our survival."

"So Mr. Slayne has told me. But I must be honest. I'm not pleased at how he dragged me from my office and forced me to accompany him whether I wanted to or not."

"We talked this all out when I came to New York to meet you. I made everything plain."

"Please, Mr. Carpenter. Don't be condescending. You came to New York for the specific purpose of recruiting me. You persuaded me to become part of your Endworld Protocol, as you call it. But my heart was never in it and you knew that." Deepak indicated Slayne. "That's why you sent your pit bull."

Slayne arched an eyebrow. "You're *alive*, aren't you? A lot aren't. Count your blessings."

"Yes, yes, I appreciate that fact," Deepak assured him. "But this is still hard for me. I wasn't given time to say good-bye to my parents. I wasn't permitted to go home and get some things I would dearly love to have brought. I was shanghaied, for lack of a better word. And I resent that."

Carpenter leaned back and made a tent of his fingers. "I'm sorry to hear it. I truly am. If you feel that strongly, you can leave."

"Just like that?" Deepak snapped his fingers.

"No one is forced to stay against his or her will. But I warn you, the initial stages of the war have been mild compared to what is to come. So far the superpowers have been content with launching a few select strikes. But all-out war will soon begin, and when it does, few outside the walls of this compound will be safe."

"You exaggerate. Not every city in America will be nuked. Many rural areas will get little if any fallout. There's the military with Cheyenne Mountain and the like, and those who have their own shelters. Plus all those who live in remote regions." Deepak shook his head. "Many millions will be perfectly safe."

"You're forgetting the biological and chemical weapons." Carpenter sought to set him straight. "Don't think they won't be used, treaties or no treaties. Once they are, life beyond these walls will become a hell we can't imagine."

"I have a good imagination," Deepak said dryly.

"It sounds to me as if you could use some rest. Or would you like a hot meal first?"

Alf Richardson rubbed his belly. "Did I hear food? Mister, lead me to the trough. All we've had the whole trip were candy bars and beef jerky. I am so hungry for real food I'd eat a cow raw." He stood and poked Deepak. "Come on, buddy. Let's go."

Deepak rose and turned to go. "Don't misunderstand. I appreciate the extra effort you went to on my behalf. But we have important matters to discuss later."

"As you wish."

The moment the door closed behind them, Patrick Slayne sighed. "What's up with him? He's been like that the whole way."

Carpenter held up a finger, pressed a button, and said into an intercom, "Becca, would you kindly show Mr. Kapur and his friend around? Whatever they need, see that they get it."

"Of course, sir."

Carpenter sat back. "Do you remember when we first met, Patrick? I made an appointment to meet with you and explained my plans for the compound? I wanted to hire the best there were to do the designs and oversee the construction, and you went one step further. You wanted to be part of the Endworld Protocol, and I made you Chief of Home Security."

"I knew war was inevitable."

"I felt the same. Which is why this compound exists. But as Mr. Kapur just pointed out, he never fully believed. Oh, I convinced him to sign on, but I could tell he might prove to be a bother later on."

"Then why waste your energy? Why didn't you recruit someone else to do what he does?"

"For the same reason I went to your firm. I wanted the best, and what that man doesn't know about computers and their operating systems isn't worth knowing."

"Still," Slayne said, "I saw his file, remember? Diana says he could cause disharmony in the group." Slayne paused. "Where is she, by the way? Did she make it?"

"As a matter of fact, Dr. Trevor arrived late last night. She was suffering from exhaustion, but otherwise she's fine. As for Mr. Kapur, I admit his psych profile is borderline. But in time I expect him to come around to our way of thinking."

Slayne gestured at the computer on Carpenter's desk. "How much use do you expect to get out of him, anyhow?"

"You tell me. You oversaw our EMP shielding. Plus we have enough fuel for our generators to last years."

"All right. Enough about him. Where do we stand with personnel? How many have checked in?"

"The total stands at ninety-seven. We're missing three singles. The fifteen couples and their families all arrived safely, thank goodness. They're the core. The last to show up was Soren Anderson and his family, about nine o'clock this morning."

"The construction guy?"

Carpenter nodded. "We have a bigger worry. I've lost contact with Ben Thomas. The last we heard from him, he was stopping at a place called Smelterville."

"You should have left that to me instead of sending me

after Kapur. Relying on a freelance was asking for trouble."

"Thomas came highly recommended. I made a judgment call. Don't be offended."

"After all you spent on the SEAL."

"I know. I know. It's critically important that we have it. I pray to God Thomas shows up."

"God?" Slayne said and indulged in a rare grin. "Haven't you been listening to the news? God is on vacation. The devil is running things."

"Ironic, isn't it?"

"What is? The end of the world? That we were smart enough to see it coming but too stupid to stop it?"

"It's ironic that for all our accomplishments, for all our sophistication and culture, our arts and science and engineering, we shoot ourselves in the head with our hate."

"What's so sophisticated about a species that can't get along? You don't see dolphins nuking each other."

Carpenter chuckled, and rose. "I suppose you want to eat and rest after your long drive."

"No. I want to take a look around. I can sleep after the war is over."

"We'll take that look together. I need to stretch my legs."

They emerged from C Block into a chill gust of wind. Roiling black clouds darkened the horizon. In the far distance vivid streaks of lightning lanced the firmament.

"Just what we need," Kurt Carpenter said.

Various vehicles were parked in rows near the inner moat on the west side of the compound. The drawbridge was down and would stay down until Carpenter gave the order for lockdown. Scores of people were milling about or clustered in small groups and talking in hushed tones. Many fidgeted and cast anxious glances at the heavens.

"They know it won't be long."

Carpenter stared at the gathering storm. "I hope to God I don't get them killed."

"It's a little late to second-guess yourself."

"I know. But I'm human, aren't I? I shudder to think what will happen if we haven't covered every contingency."

Slayne put a hand on his shoulder. "Relax. You've thought of everything. From food stockpiles to weapons and ammo to radiation gear to biohazard suits, we're as prepared as we can be."

A small yellow ball rolled toward them and stopped near their feet. A little girl followed it. She scooped it up, then saw Carpenter and froze as if transfixed. Her mother hurried over and took her by the shoulders.

"Sorry to disturb you, Mr. Carpenter."

"That's quite all right, Mrs. Reynolds." Carpenter noticed with amusement that they kept looking at him as they walked off. "What on earth was that all about?"

From behind them came a contralto female voice. "You're the Great Prophet. They hold you in awe."

Both men turned. "Professor Trevor!" Carpenter smiled warmly and embraced her. "I expected you to sleep until evening."

"It's the end of the world as we know it. I don't want to miss any more than I absolutely have to." Diana had on a clean green blouse and jeans. She held out her hand. "Patrick."

Slayne shook it. "Diana."

"I'm glad to see you made it."

"I had special incentive."

"Anyone I know?"

Slayne looked into her eyes. "Looked in a mirror today?"

"Come see me tonight. We'll look in it together."

Kurt Carpenter cleared his throat. "What was that nonsense about my being held in awe? I trust you were joking."

"Look around you. Haven't you noticed the stares? Or how nervous they are around you?" Diana swept an arm toward the drawbridge and the walls. "This is all your doing. You're the mastermind, the guiding genius. This place wouldn't exist except for you. They look up to you. They revere you. And yes, some even hold you in awe."

"That's ridiculous."

"It's human nature."

Carpenter began to reply, but just then Slayne's cell jingled. "Excuse me." He moved to one side and answered it.

"Hello, Arthur. Yes, this might be our last contact for a while. The atmospheric disturbance will be severe and we can't predict how long it will last. Stick to the plan. Get to Switzerland, to the shelter under the chateau. Stay there until it's over, and if you can, take up the reins. Yes, yes, try to contact me then. With any luck at all—" Slayne stopped. "Arthur? Arthur?"

"Who was that?" Diana asked.

"Arthur Banning, Vice President of Tekco. He was in London on a stopover. The line went dead."

Carpenter said, "It's amazing he even got through." A gust of wind struck Carpenter, drawing his gaze to the approaching thunderhead. "Say. Do either of you notice anything strange about that storm front?"

Slayne and Diana looked.

"What are those flashes of light high up in the clouds? See them? The purple and green that comes and goes. That's not lightning." Carpenter turned to Slayne. "Would you be so kind as to get everyone into their assigned bunkers and then join me in C Block?"

"Consider it done."

Diana watched Slayne hurry off. "Ever notice how he moves? Just like a leopard or a jaguar."

Carpenter's mouth curved. "No, I can't say as I have."

"It's about to hit the fan, isn't it? The moment you've been waiting for."

"The moment I've been dreading, Diana. All I've done, all my preparations, are about to be put to the test, and I honestly don't know if it's enough."

A purple streak lit the sky, but there was no boom of thunder. The wind began to whistle and shriek.

Carpenter watched his followers scurry for cover. "These people have put their lives in my hands. What if I get them killed?"

"Didn't I hear Patrick say something about not second-guessing yourself? You've done all you can. Now we ride it out and pray for the best."

"I thought you were agnostic?"

"What's that old saying? In a foxhole—and when the world comes to an end—there aren't any agnostics or atheists. There are only believers, wetting themselves."

Carpenter gave the world a last scrutiny. The end of days had come. He supposed he should feel pleased his dire predictions had proven true but it was hard to get excited over what might prove to be the death knell of an entire planet. "How could we do this to ourselves?"

The dark clouds and the purple flashes now filled half the sky and swept toward the compound like a swarm of ethereal demons.

Slayne was hastening a few stragglers toward the bunkers. "A penny for your thoughts?"

"You can have them for free, Diana." Carpenter nodded at the atmospheric upheaval. "The human race has rolled the dice on its existence, and the dice have come up snake eyes."

Havoc In A-Major

Minnesota

It had long been reasoned, by sane and reasonable men who assumed that the majority of their fellow humans were equally sane and reasonable, that no one in his or her right mind wanted nuclear war. Nukes were a deterrent. They kept tyrants from overstepping the accepted bounds of tyranny. They kept despots from spreading the borders of their despotism. They kept nations from waging all-out war on other nations.

To these sane and reasonable men, this had seemed a sane and reasonable system. It had worked for so long—admittedly, not perfectly—but reasonably well, enough that planet Earth had enjoyed an extended period of relative peace and global prosperity.

Toward the end, more and more countries had acquired more and more nukes. The superpowers, those who had had nukes first and hoarded them as they hoarded gold on the theory that an enemy who was afraid of one nuke would be terrified of ten thousand, built their stockpiles to a point where they were perfectly happy to sign treaties that forced them to dismantle a few each year, after which they would have 9,997 left.

But since envy holds true for nukes as much as it does for fancy cars and palatial homes, the little countries had seen how smug the big countries were behind their wall of nuclear deterrence, and they wanted deterrents of their own. So it wasn't long before a dozen small countries had nukes.

Only one country on the whole face of the planet had developed a nuclear program out of necessity. Israel's survival depended on nukes its government denied having, but they didn't mind one bit when word of the secret hoard was "accidentally" leaked and the country's enemies found out about the weapons.

At the outset of Armageddon, no one had known the exact number of nukes in existence. Experts had said that this or that country possessed this or that many, but the experts had been doing what experts always did when they didn't know, yet were being paid to pretend they did: they blew wind. The truth was that keeping complete and accurate track of the manufacture and development of all the components that went into the making of a nuclear bomb or missile, from the plutonium to the housing, was impossible. So the experts had given their best guesses, and those who paid them had been content.

It didn't help that the experts vehemently disagreed. One had said the total was 27,304. Another had said that that was preposterous, and there were only 10,563. Still another had claimed that surely the total tally of warheads must exceed 50,000.

Kurt Carpenter hadn't trusted any of the assessments. All that mattered to him was there were a lot of nuclear weapons, and when the next world war came, odds were that a lot of them would be used.

That wasn't all.

Biological and chemical weapons had become all the political rage. Treaties had been signed to limit their production, usually with public fanfare so the politicians who signed the treaties would be perceived as great humanitarians. But those same politicians had required their militaries to secretly develop new and ever more lethal stockpiles. Just in case, had been their mantra.

There had also been reports of even more exotic weapons. Weapons spun from the pages of science fiction. Devices so terrible, they were spoken of in hushed whispers behind locked doors.

Kurt Carpenter had done the math, and the conclusion he'd reached was that the next global war would result in horrors the likes of which had never been seen.

But Carpenter did his math a little differently from most.

The common consensus had been that if X number of nuclear bombs and missiles were set off, it would result in Y amount of destruction and Z amount of radiation.

The common consensus had been that if bio weapons were used, they would do what they were designed to do—induce disease, shrivel the brain so it resembled a fig, produce a quantifiable number of fatalities, and that would be that.

The same with chemical weapons. The victims would die, screaming in agony while their skin burned off or they broke out in cancerous boils or their lungs tried to claw out of their chests, and then the catalyzing agents would break down, and that would be that.

Carpenter didn't see it that way. To him each type of weapon and the results it produced weren't necessarily distinct and separate. Carpenter didn't see them as one, two, and three. Oh, the effects produced by one, two, and three were well documented when each was tested alone. But what happened when one, two, and three interacted? What was the consequence when, say, a bio weapon or a chemical weapon was employed in a zone of high radioactivity from a nearby nuclear strike? What did mixing one and two add up to? What did mixing two and three? Or one and three? Or one, two, and three? No research had been done on the cumulative consequences. Did radiation alter the chemical components of chemical weapons? When a biological weapon and a chemical weapon were used on the same battlefield, did their combined effects bring about something more—and worse—than their horrific individual effects?

No one really knew. The few scientists who had given the scenario any attention admitted that the variables were beyond them. They could theorize. They could create computer models. But those models were only as good as the information fed into the computers, and that was woefully sparse. Yes, nuclear weapons had been used before. Yes, bio weapons and chemical weapons had been used before. But the three had never been used at the same time.

Carpenter had taken all the precautions he could. The site he had chosen was located far enough from military and civilian targets that fallout should be minimal. Internal air circulation and filtration systems minimized the risk of bio and chemical weapons. Hazard suits and other gear would protect them when they had to venture outdoors.

Was it enough? That was the question eating at Kurt Carpenter when he imposed lockdown. The three missing members still hadn't shown up, and the SEAL still hadn't been delivered.

That troubled him greatly. He'd invested millions in the special vehicle's development and manufacture. It had been designed to operate in a post-apocalyptic environment. Solar powered, it could navigate any terrain and even cruise on water if it had to. With enough firepower to take out a regiment, the SEAL was his way of insuring that the Family would survive the brave new world in which it found itself.

But he couldn't wait any longer for it to arrive.

Events in the outside world had reached the point where it was time for those he had gathered together to retreat into their concrete shells.

On a cloudy, chilly afternoon, Carpenter called the Family together and announced that he was imposing lockdown. They were to stay in their assigned bunkers until he gave the all-clear to return to the surface. "I can't say how long that will be," he solemnly informed them. "There are too many variables involved. But remember, we can withstand anything short of a direct nuclear strike. You'll be perfectly safe."

"Until we come back up," someone said.

At a command from Slayne, everyone dispersed. Within minutes the bunker doors were sealed, the compound empty of human life.

Beyond the walls, World War Three raged in all of its global fury.

Carpenter spent every moment he could in the Communications Center. At considerable expense he had installed state-of-the-art receiving units covering the complete broadcast spectrum, everything from satellite to citizens band. He'd also had his tech people set up a powerful transmitter and a backup.

At first it was fairly easy to follow the unfolding conflict. Hostilities were confined to the Middle East as long-held animosities spilled over. The spark came when Israel invaded Lebanon and stayed. Iran, Iraq, and Egypt, with China's backing, retaliated. The Russians entered the fray, taking advantage of the confusion to clamp down on neighboring countries. One thing led to another and the United States sent in a task force, only to have the ships and personnel obliterated by a nuke.

After that, the pace of death-dealing quickened. China, Russia, the United States, the Koreas, England, France, Japan, even Australia were all drawn in.

It truly was a *world* war.

Tel Aviv, Tehran, and Cairo were nuked. The Vatican went up in a radioactive cloud. The Turks and the Greeks went at it yet again. They didn't have nukes, but they did have chemical weapons. Crete, or rather the people on it, ceased to exist. India and Pakistan lobbed missiles at each other, and when the dust settled, it settled on heaps of dead.

In the United States, San Diego was hit. Conflicting reports said the same about Seattle and San Francisco.

There was no doubt about New York City. Slayne, Kapur, and Richardson had seen it with their own eyes.

The U.S. government held off using its own arsenal until New York was turned into a Roman candle. Why they waited so long, Carpenter couldn't say, unless they were marshaling for a counterstrike on multiple fronts. But when Manhattan was blasted into oblivion, the American military juggernaut was given the command to kill, and kill they did. In an hour, newscasts carried accounts of U.S. nuclear strikes on targets in the Middle East, China, and North Korea. The latter was especially hard hit; every major North Korean city was now rubble.

Reports on Russia were mixed. Some claimed the Russians were fighting with American forces against the Chinese and their Arabian satraps. Other reports claimed the Russians were in Canada and had also landed in Philadelphia.

Carpenter couldn't begin to fathom why the Russians would attack the U.S. homeland, or why they would choose the City of Brotherly Love—unless some general high in the Kremlin loved irony.

In America, chaos spread like a Kansas prairie fire. Riots broke out in dozens of cities and towns. The National Guard was mobilized, but with so many Guard units overseas they were stretched too thin. There was little they could do to stem the rising tidal wave of civil unrest. It was like plugging a hole in a dyke with a finger while cracks radiated outward, growing larger and larger until finally the dyke burst.

The president's call for calm fell on deaf ears. Declaring martial law likewise did little to stem the panic.

The dogs of war had been unleashed and the hounds were in full bray.

A map of the United States covered one wall of the Com Center. Carpenter had his staff stick pins in it. Red pins for cities hit by nukes, orange pins for cites and towns where rioting and looting was known to have occurred, green pins for cities where the authorities had things pretty much in hand. There were precious few green pins.

The staff soon added more colors. Yellow for areas where chemical weapons had been used. Brown pins for bio weapons. There were few of those because it was largely based on guesswork that stemmed from news accounts of people breaking out in sores or shuffling like the living dead.

At one point Becca Levy bowed her head, closed her eyes, and groaned. "How can we do this to ourselves?"

Diana overheard. "I could go into the finer points of the psychology of destruction. Or the alleged human need for misery. But I won't. The plain and simple truth is that men and women have been killing one another since the dawn of recorded time."

"But *why?*" Becca persisted. "What is it that brings out the animal in us?"

"The animal in us," Diana said. "With apologies to animals everywhere."

"What? Oh, I get it. You're saying it's innate. Like our need to breathe and to reproduce." Becca shook her head. "Sorry, Professor. But I'm not buying it. There's more to us than claws and teeth. We feel. We think. We reason."

Diana nodded at a speaker on the wall. A radio announcer was reciting a list of cities that no longer existed. "We slaughter one another on an unprecedented scale."

"Shhhhh, you two." Carpenter had caught a mention of the Twin Cities. He motioned for the technician to boost the gain.

> *". . . surprisingly quiet. Some looting was reported, but the authorities have it under control. There hasn't been any of the mass mayhem reported from other urban centers."*

Carpenter nodded in satisfaction. One of the first areas they would visit, once it was safe, was Minneapolis and St. Paul.

> *"Los Angeles is reported to be in meltdown, not from a nuke but from the complete collapse of law and order. There is word that street gangs now control whole sections of the city."*

"Switch to military frequencies," Carpenter directed. He still hoped, feebly, that U.S. military might would prevail and the war would end with a decisive U.S. victory. But given the nature and scope of the hostilities, it was more than likely that no one would win, that the war would devolve into a stalemate, or, worse, that it would bring about the complete and utter collapse of every nation on the globe, plunging the world into a new and terrifying Dark Age.

The speaker crackled with static. It hummed. It squawked. Suddenly a shrill voice blared.

> *"Mayday! Mayday! Air Force One is going down! Repeat: Air Force One is going down! We are fifty air miles out of Colorado Springs. I can see a mushroom cloud. Our exact—"*

The transmission died.

Carpenter turned to the tech. "Can you get that back?"

"I'm trying. Hold on, sir."

"Call me Kurt, Miriem. No one is to call me sir. We're a Family, not the army or navy."

"There's nothing, si—Kurt."

"On that channel?"

"On any of the channels."

"Switch back to the civilian bands, then. Radio will do. AM or FM, it doesn't matter."

"You don't understand. There's nothing at all. Anywhere. No AM No FM. No military. No satellite. It's all gone."

"I was afraid of this."

Miriem tweaked knobs, flipped switches and pressed buttons. "There should be *something*. All I get is silence. Everywhere. As if the whole world has been wiped out."

"You can stop trying," Carpenter advised. "Saturation has occurred."

"What?" Diana asked.

"You're familiar with the EMP effect? Yes. Well, most studies dealt with the effect of a single strategic nuclear blast. Few delved into the repercussions of ten warheads going off at about the same time. Or fifty. Or a hundred. But one study I saw did just that. The scientist who wrote it hypothesized a saturation effect, where so many nukes go off that nothing gets through."

"How long will it last?"

"No telling. It could be months or even years." Carpenter sat back. "We're completely cut off from the outside world."

"God help us," Becca Levy said.

Brave New World

They stayed in the bunker for thirty days and thirty nights. They could have stayed longer. They were stocked with enough food and water and other supplies to sustain themselves for years.

Based on the compound's location and prevailing winds, the experts Carpenter had consulted determined that little fallout from U.S. targets would reach them. And since radiation decayed exponentially, those same experts concluded that it would be safe for Carpenter and his followers to emerge from their reinforced bunkers three to five weeks after the war ended.

Carpenter wanted to be the first one out, but Patrick Slayne wouldn't hear of it. "I'm chief of security so the risk is rightfully mine. Besides, we can't afford to lose you. You built this place. You got all these people together. They look up to you. If you die it would devastate them."

Diana Trevor agreed. "Like it or not, Patrick is right.

You're the leader. As much as you might want to, you can't take unnecessary risks."

Reluctantly, Carpenter gave in.

Slayne donned a type of hazmat suit used by the military. Known as an NBC suit—or Nuclear, Biological, Chemical suit—it was hard for civilians to obtain. Slayne's status as CEO of Tekco had overcome that hurdle. The suit was fully sealed and had radiation shielding. It was a Level A, which meant it closed the wearer off completely from the outside world. To breathe, Slayne relied on a respirator strapped to his back.

Slayne picked up a Geiger counter. While some models measured gamma and beta radiation, this one also measured alpha. The sensor was the most sensitive on the market.

Slayne nodded at the others and climbed the ladder to the trapdoor that separated the underground levels from the upper levels. He went to the airlock, went through the inner door, and closed it behind him. He worked the wheel to the outer door and pushed. The heavy door swung easily on recessed pivots. Through his faceplate, he glimpsed the high walls and the moat.

The Com link buzzed and Carpenter's voice blared in his ears. "Are you outside yet? What do you see?"

"I'm tying my shoes," Slayne quipped. "And don't shout. I can hear you just fine."

"Sorry. I'm a little nervous. I don't want anything to happen to you, Patrick. I rely on you more than you realize."

"You'd do just fine without me." Slayne meant it. One of the things that had impressed him when he first met Carpenter was the man's attention to detail.

Nothing, no matter how trivial, escaped him. Even on subjects he knew little about, he intuitively asked questions that brought out the most pertinent information.

"Don't even joke about a thing like that."

"Quiet now. I'm going out. I'll contact you when I have something to report."

Slayne pushed the door all the way open and strode outside. A gust buffeted him. The sky was strange, gray instead of blue with periodic flashes of light. It lent a preternatural twilight to everything. All else appeared normal. Kneeling, he ran his gloved fingers through the grass but found no dust from fallout.

The Geiger chirped when Slayne turned it on. He adjusted it for maximum gain and began his sweeps, keeping a close eye on the meter. He went all the way to the moat. The readings were only slightly higher than normal, interrupted here and there by a random spike from a hot particle brought in by the wind.

Slayne climbed the steps over the moat to the rampart on the west wall. Woodland stretched for as far as the eye could see. Undisturbed, pristine, serene.

Looking at it, one would never guess that a month ago the world had been in the grip of all-out war. He was about to climb back down when he gave a start and faced the woods. He tapped his helmet to be sure his pickup was working properly. It was.

There was no sound. The wind had died, and the woods were utterly silent.

Slayne boosted the volume to max. Still nothing, save an eerie, somber stillness. It was if he were listening to a dead world. An earth stripped of life and left empty.

Again Slayne went to descend. But at the edge of his faceplate he caught a movement on a low rise to the southeast. A dark silhouette was framed against the gray sky. All Slayne could tell was that the figure had two legs.

He raised his left arm and waved, but the figure didn't wave back. It just stood there a bit longer, then melted into the trees.

His helmet crackled.

"Damn it, Patrick. How long are you going to keep me waiting? Are you all right? Is it safe or not?"

"Bring the kiddies and have a picnic."

"Be serious."

"I am."

Carpenter wasn't satisfied. Each bunker had two hazmat suits, and over the next several days, teams went over every square yard of the thirty-acre compound. The air was tested. The water in the moat was tested. The soil was tested. Finally Carpenter had to admit the obvious.

"It's safe enough. But I'm still uneasy. We'll let small groups go out for a few hours at a time."

"Guards need to be posted on the walls," Slayne said. "I'll break open the armory and pass out weapons to the men I choose."

"Actually," Carpenter said, "I have an idea along those lines. Let's see. It's Wednesday. On Sunday we'll have the first official gathering of our Family and I'll detail my plans."

"You never have told me why you keep calling us that."

"On Sunday, Patrick. On Sunday."

Everyone was excited at the prospect of going outside. Anxious, too, since no one knew what to expect. They accepted that it was safe—but for how long? Doomsday had occurred. Even though they had hoped to survive, the fact that they had was no small miracle, and for some, it was difficult to wrap their minds around.

Diana Trevor wasn't surprised by their reaction. It was a common enough psychological phenomenon. Survivors of disasters were often bewildered and emotionally numb. She cautioned Carpenter to take things slow and give his charges time to adjust to their new reality.

It didn't help that nearly everyone had been bombarded

with the media's dire predictions. Fallacies had been paraded as fact and accepted by the public at large.

Carpenter addressed the issue. An intercom system linked the bunkers, and it was his habit to speak a few words of encouragement before retiring. This night his subject was the aftermath of the war.

"Let's take a look at some of the claims that were made. First, that everyone on the planet would die. Realistic projections were that the war would kill 20 percent of the human race in the first few days. Another forty to fifty percent would die from radiation poisoning, starvation, violence, what have you. That still leaves billions. Yes, you heard that right. *Billions.*

"Another claim was that lethal radiation would blanket the earth for centuries. But our compound only received a small amount, and many other areas received as little or none at all. In other words, whole regions are as habitable now as they were before the bombs were dropped.

"It was claimed that no crops would grow and that all vegetation would wither and die. But the grass and the trees here are fine, and are undoubtedly fine elsewhere. Think of the Amazon, or the taiga of Russia and northern Canada. Think of the vast tracts of the United States where there were no military targets. Other than fallout, they are untouched, and will go on as they have been for countless ages.

"The point of all this is to soothe your fears. Yes, we must take precautions. Yes, we must be on our guard when we are outside the walls. We can't drink or eat anything unless we know it is safe. But overall, all things considered, we are doing fine."

The next morning Patrick Slayne needed two men to help him make a quick walk-through of the compound. He chose Soren Anderson and Alf Richardson.

Richardson wasn't an official member of the group but when he heard Slayne ask Anderson, he eagerly volunteered to come along.

"I'm tired of being cooped up. I want to feel the sun on my face and breathe real air again."

Slayne conducted them to the armory. He chose an MP5 fitted with a shoulder strap. It was compact and held a 30-round magazine. For a sidearm he selected an Astra A-75, in 9mm. He was strapping on the holster when he looked up and saw the other two standing there, staring at him. "What are you waiting for? I recommend a pistol or revolver, and either a rifle or an SMG."

"SM-what?" Alf said.

"Submachine gun." Slayne patted the MP5.

Alf gawked at the racks of weapons. "Where did you get so many? There must be hundreds."

"There are," Slayne with a trace of pride. "I picked every one. Kurt wanted a wide variety, and we have guns from just about everywhere. A lot of other weapons, too, like knives and swords. Even a genuine tomahawk."

"I don't know what to take," Alf confessed. "I know as much about guns as I do about physics."

"I'll help." Slayne turned to Anderson. "What about you?"

Soren held up Mjolnir. "This will do."

"A hammer?" Slayne repressed a grin. "I understand you're in construction, but isn't that carrying it a bit far? A hammer against a gun will lose every time."

"This isn't a tool." Soren held it out so they could see the intricate detail and the runes. "This is Mjolnir, the special weapon of the God of Thunder." He hefted it so the light played over its massive head. "It's the best replica ever made."

Slayne looked at him. "It's *still* just a hammer. If you

want to take it, fine. Stick it under your belt. But you need a gun, and that's final."

Soren didn't argue. Slayne was responsible for the safety of the compound and the welfare of their loved ones. He would do as the man wanted. But Alf Richardson was right; there were so many.

Soren had fired guns when he was younger, but he wasn't an expert. He knew a .45 used a bigger bullet than a .22, but that was about it. He walked past several racks until he came to one with a sign that read SHOTGUNS. Soren's grandfather had owned a fine double-barreled shotgun, and Soren had gotten to shoot it a few times. It had taught him the truth of the statement that a shotgun was the next best thing to a cannon.

One in particular caught Soren's eye. It was shorter than the rest, and had a pistol grip instead of a stock. A label under it told him it was a Mossberg Model 500 12-gauge. It came with a sling, which would free his hands to use Mjolnir if need be. He took it down and tried to work the slide but it wouldn't budge. Closer inspection revealed a stud under the breech. Printed next to it was Release Lever with Thumb Only. Soren pressed the lever and jacked the slide and it worked fine.

In a drawer under the rack were boxes of ammunition. He had his choice of slugs, buckshot, or birdshot. Folded with the boxes were several bandoleers.

He helped himself to one and filled half its loops with slugs and the other half with buckshot. Then he rejoined the others.

"What do you think?" Alf Richardson asked, and grinned uncertainly. Two semiautomatics were strapped to his ample waist and he clutched a bolt-action rifle. "This is a .30-06, whatever that is. Mr. Slayne says I can drop just about anything with it."

"Remember to aim like I told you." Slayne had debated giving him an SMG but the man was a bundle of nerves. He could just see Richardson panicking and cutting loose with the SMG on full auto, taking down friend as well as foe.

Soren showed him the shotgun. "Is this all right?"

"Whatever you feel comfortable with. But if you load it with double-ought, don't fire anywhere in our direction."

Nodding, Soren fed slugs into the magazine and pumped a round into the chamber.

They went out through the door instead of the airlock. The somber gray sky gave both Soren and Alf pause.

Slayne had brought a Geiger counter. He took readings and informed them the radiation levels were no higher than last time.

"Spread out and we'll have a look around."

"What are we looking for?" Alf asked. "It's not as if anyone or anything can get in here with the drawbridge up."

"We make sure anyway. I want you to climb up on the wall and see how things look. Mr. Anderson, if you would be so kind, patrol the perimeter of the moat and check for tracks."

Slayne started on a circuit of the concrete bunkers, which were arranged in a triangle.

Soren did as he was told. He walked to the north until he came to the edge of the moat and then bore to the east. The steep bank was thick with grass and wouldn't bear tracks well. He stopped once he was out of Slayne's sight, slung the Mossberg over his shoulder, and slid Mjolnir from under his belt. He felt more comfortable using the hammer than the shotgun. He went on and abruptly realized how deathly still it was. There should have been birds chirping, squirrels chattering, insects buzzing. But there was nothing—nothing at all—save the gurgle of the water and occasional spurts of wind.

Over at the bunkers, Slayne had passed B Block and was nearing C. He saw no reason for alarm and decided that as soon as Soren got back he would let Kurt know it was safe to send up surface parties.

"Mr. Slayne! Mr. Slayne! Up here!"

On the west rampart, Alf was hopping up and down and waving.

Slayne wondered if he had seen a deer. Amused by his little joke, he hurried to the stairs and climbed to Alf's side. "This better be important."

"You would know better than me." Alf pointed. "Is that what I think it is?"

Attached to the top of the wall was a grappling hook.

First Blood

Patrick Slayne saw the grappling hook and remembered the figure he had seen silhouetted against the sky. He put two and two together and came up with extreme danger. He whirled.

A man in jeans and a T-shirt was crouched on the inner bank of the moat. He had a rifle. Even as Slayne spun, the man fired.

The rifle was a Weatherby. The caliber was .340 Magnum. The slug, traveling at 3,260 feet per second when it left the muzzle, cored Alf Richardson's head from front to back before Alf could blink. It entered squarely in the center of his forehead and burst out the rear of his cranium with such explosive force, much of his skull and a lot of his brain were splattered over the rampart. The last sound he heard was the thunder of the shot. The last sight he saw was the gray sky as his head was snapped back.

Patrick Slayne dived flat, rolled, and came up into a crouch with the MP5 tucked at his side. He didn't need to aim. He fired on full auto and stitched the man from crotch to throat.

Another rifle opened up, from a corner of C Block, and then two more, from behind other bunkers.

Slayne dived flat again, swearing at himself for his carelessness. He'd liked the simple, sincere, and eager-to-please Alf. It was why he hadn't tossed Alf out of the Hunster that first day in New York City.

A slug whined off the wall, reminding Slayne he couldn't afford to make the same mistake twice. He wondered where Soren Anderson had gotten to and hoped the man wouldn't do anything stupid like rush out into the open and get himself shot. He frowned as he remembered that Soren had chosen a shotgun. Shotguns were fine at close range but as useful as slingshots at any great distance. He risked a peek to see if he could spot Soren and nearly lost an eye.

One of the hostiles could shoot.

At that moment, Soren was sprinting back along the north arm of the moat. He didn't know what was going on. At first he had thought it was Alf, shooting for some reason. But then he heard the submachine gun and more rifles. A pitched battle was taking place. But who was the enemy?

Soren gave no thought to his safety. His friends needed his help. He was staring toward the bunkers and the west wall of the moat, and he almost missed spotting the man in a flannel shirt crouched behind an oak not thirty feet away. He threw himself headlong just as the bolt-action rifle the man was aiming went off.

Soren cut loose with the Mossberg, pumping twice. The slugs hit the tree, not the man, but caused him to jerk back. Soren heaved to his knees to take better aim. He saw the man tugging frantically at the bolt. His rifle had somehow jammed.

Soren acted without thinking. He let the Mossberg

swing at his side by the shoulder sling, and was up and running toward the stranger, as fast as he could run. As he charged he yanked Mjolnir free of his belt and held the heavy hammer in both hands.

The man was still tugging. He heard Soren's footfalls and glanced up.

"No!"

By then Soren was on him. He swung Mjolnir in an arc. Flesh and bone were no match for metal; a third of the man's skull became pulp.

Soren didn't linger. He raced toward the Blocks and spotted another man at the rear corner of C Block, firing up at the west wall. The man's back was to him.

Soren pumped his legs, hoping the boom of gunfire would drown out the slap of his boots.

The shooter had a lever-action rifle and was firing spaced shots. Suddenly he stiffened and half turned.

Soren had only ten feet to go. He covered it in two long bounds. The rifle went off, but if he was hit he didn't feel anything. He swung at the man's forearm and heard a *crack*. The man screamed and sought to flee, but Soren swung again, slamming Mjolnir against the side of the man's head.

There was no need to confirm the man was dead, not when one eyeball was where his nose should be.

Soren ran on, but cautiously. As best he could tell, two more riflemen were firing from somewhere south of him. It puzzled him that he didn't hear Alf and Slayne shoot back. He came to the far corner of C Block, stopped, and peeked out.

Up on the rampart, Patrick Slayne had set his gun selector from full auto to three-round burst. Now he reared up just high enough to trigger a trio of leaden hornets at a man who had been shooting at him from behind B Block.

The man ducked back, and Slayne dropped flat again. Soren realized Slayne and Alf had been pinned down.

One hundred yards separated C Block from B Block but Soren didn't hesitate. He raced toward B Block. The rifleman was at the far end, the south end, so there was every chance the man wouldn't spot him. Still, he prickled with the expectation of taking a slug. Relief washed over him when he reached the north wall. As careful as could be, he peered around the corner.

The man was at the other corner, looking up at the west rampart, his back to Soren.

Soren went to reach for the shotgun but changed his mind. Mjolnir hadn't failed him yet. With a silent prayer to Odin, he slipped from concealment and ran in a crouch.

The man fired another shot.

Soren was close enough to see him clearly. An older man, hair streaked with gray, his chin covered with stubble. Around his waist was a cartridge belt. The rifle was another bolt-action. Soren had no idea what kind it was.

Up on the wall, the SMG burped.

Soren shut all thought from his mind and firmed his grip on Mjolnir. Moving slowly now, making no sound whatsoever, he came up behind the man and raised Mjolnir over his head. He almost uttered a war cry but remembered that there was at least one more enemy to deal with. Instead, he said quietly, "Give my regards to the Valkyries."

The man glanced around. Fear twisted his features, and he tried to bring his rifle to bear.

Soren swept Mjolnir down with all his might. The *splat*, the blood, the dead husk at his feet were nothing compared to the tingling sensation that shot through him, as if he had gripped a live electrical wire by mistake. It was a sensation he had only ever felt twice before: once when he slew the last gangsta; and again when he slew the looter. It was exquisite beyond belief, a feeling of raw potent power such as he had imagined only in his wildest fantasies. He attributed it to one source. Holding Mjolnir aloft, he gazed at the gray sky and said with fiery passion, "Lord Thor, I thank you!"

The bang of a rifle brought Soren back to the here and now. There was that one foe yet to deal with.

The last invader was at the near corner of A Block. He was firing at the west wall, but he was facing B Block.

It would be impossible for Soren to reach him unseen. He pondered what to do. He could try the shotgun, but he wasn't sure he could hit him. He needed to get closer. But how? He glanced behind him at the man he had just laid low, and he grinned. Bending, he dragged the body close to the corner and positioned it so that only part of a shoulder and one arm showed. Then, squatting with his back to the wall, he covered his mouth with his left hand to muffle the sound and let out with a long, loud groan. He waited, then repeated it. He waited some more, and taking a chance, he mouthed a muffled, "Help me!" Then he jiggled the arm that stuck past the corner, careful not to show his own hand when he did it.

A rifle *spanged* once, twice, three times, and feet thudded in swift cadence, drawing closer.

The rifleman came flying around the corner. He was looking down at the body. "Frank? Where were you hit?"

Soren was ready. He swept Mjolnir up and around and caught the man full in the face. The impact lifted the invader off his feet and stretched him out flat on his back with his life's blood gushing from his shattered mouth and nose and seeping from his eye sockets. The man gasped and gulped and struggled for breath, his fingers clawing for the rifle he had dropped.

"In Thor's name," Soren said, and brought Mjolnir crashing down. He stared at his handiwork, then stepped back and shook the bloody hammer to rid it of its gore.

No more shots pealed. No shouts rose.

Soren peered around the bunker. He saw no other riflemen but he needed to be sure. He let several minutes go by. When nothing happened, he cupped his hand to his mouth. "Alf! Slayne! Are you all right?"

Up on the rampart, Patrick Slayne swore. "Look out! Keep quiet! There are at least three of them and they have rifles!"

"There were four."

Slayne took this to mean Anderson had killed one. "Stay down, damn it! I don't want you shot!"

"There is no one left." Soren stepped from behind the Block. "It's safe to come down if you want."

Risking a quick look, Slayne saw the big construction worker standing in the open, holding his hammer.

"They're all dead," Soren said.

Slayne slowly rose partway. Could it be? he wondered. When he didn't draw lead, he stood fully erect. "They're dead, you say?"

Soren nodded.

Still not convinced, Slayne descended the stairs. He held the MP5 ready, swinging right and left, alert for movement.

Soren stayed where he was and motioned. "Back there are two of them."

"Two?" Slayne moved past and drew up short at the sight of the prone forms. He saw their brains leaking out and noticed the blood on the hammer. "Sweet Jesus."

Soren held Mjolnir high in the air. "Odin has protected and delivered us."

"You don't believe that?"

"I follow the Ancient Way, Mr. Slayne. The Way of the Elder Gods. I worship Odin. I revere Thor. If you understand nothing else about me, understand that." Soren paused. "Wait? Where's Alf?" He looked toward the west wall.

"Mr. Richardson didn't make it, I'm afraid."

"A shame. From what I saw this past month, he was a decent man."

"Mourn him when we bury him. Now we need to collect these bodies and their hardware and organize a burial detail."

Soren nudged one of them. "Who were they? Why did they try to kill us?"

"You'd have to ask them."

"It makes no sense. Why did they sneak in here and take potshots at us when they could just as easily have waited outside the walls until we saw them and then ask to be admitted?"

"I suspect they were scavengers, looking for whatever they could steal. They were probably trying to figure out how to get into the bunkers when we came out and caught them by surprise."

Voices and a commotion caused them to turn. Kurt Carpenter and five others were hurrying toward them from A Block. All except Carpenter were armed with rifles or shotguns.

"Sorry it took us so long, Patrick. The bunkers are soundproof, as you well know. If I hadn't told one of the techs to switch on an outside audio pickup, we wouldn't have known anything was wrong. We heard the shots and had to get guns and load them and—"

Slayne placed a hand on Carpenter's shoulder. "It's all right, Kurt. We'll rig cameras out here so from now on when we're in the bunkers we can see as well as hear."

Carpenter gazed about them. "I don't see Mr. Richardson."

Slayne gave an account of the clash. He stressed that Soren had had more to do with the outcome than he did.

"I'm extremely sorry to hear about Mr. Richardson. As for you, Mr. Anderson, excellent work. We must protect our own at all costs." Carpenter gave instructions to two of the others to bring shovels and picks. Then he turned back to Slayne. "A grappling hook, you say? That's how they got in?"

"Not exactly a common household item, is it? And not something a person carries around with them unless they intend to use it."

Carpenter's brow furrowed. "So they had to have known the compound was here."

"No mystery there. You had a dozen or more contractors working on your dream at one time or another. The excavation crews. The brick layers. The concrete pourers. The electricians. The plumbers. Then there are hunters and hikers who must have happened by. Throw in any locals who wondered what in God's name was going on out here, and there must be a hundred people who know where the compound is."

"And here I thought that building it in the middle of nowhere would ensure some degree of security." Carpenter sighed and regarded the dead men. "We'll see more like these, and perhaps worse. But we can't let them prevail. If we must fight for our right to exist, so be it. But let's not do it haphazardly. Just as our country had its army and navy and marines, we must do something similar."

Soren broke his silence. "Excuse me for saying so, sir, but you make it sound as if the United States no longer exists."

"It very well might not. And call me Kurt, please."

"What was that about doing something similar?" Slayne prompted.

Carpenter gazed solemnly out across the compound. "What we need, gentlemen, is a fighting force of our very own. Men and women pledged to keep intruders like these at bay." He smiled. "What we need are our very own warriors."

Sowing Seeds

Sunday dawned cloudy and chilly. Before anyone ventured outdoors, Patrick Slayne donned a hazmat suit and conducted his routine morning tests. The previous evening, he had huddled with Carpenter and Deepak Kapur and worked out how they would go about installing remote sensors on the walls. The sensors would be linked to the computers and relay radiation readings as well as the data from bio and chem sniffers.

When Slayne deemed it safe, Carpenter gave the word and everyone emerged from the six bunkers and converged on a grassy area between B Block and the moat. Carpenter encouraged them to bring food and drink and to relax and enjoy themselves, but there was an air of tension. He mentioned it to Diana Trevor, who said it was perfectly normal, given the uncertainties they faced.

Carpenter intended to set some of those uncertainties to rest. It was a few minutes before ten when he came out of C Block and stood under a maple tree, the leaves of which were turning brown earlier than they should. The buzz of conversation stopped. He smiled, then began what he believed to be the most important speech of his life.

"Good morning, brothers and sisters. For that is what we are, you know. We are all of us brothers and sisters in adversity. The greatest adversity the human race has known in modern history.

"We're not just a collection of strangers culled from all walks of life and thrown together to sink or swim as the whims of fate decide. We share a common bond, a common goal, a common need. The bond is that of survival, the goal is to continue to survive, the need is for us to continually adapt to whatever challenges our drastically changed world throws at us."

Carpenter stopped and gazed at every one of their upturned faces. "I would like to cement that bond. I would like for each of you to start thinking of those around you not as strangers but as your family." He waited for snickers or objections, but there were none.

"The Family," he repeated. "I have been calling us that for some time now. Look at the person next to you and you will see why. We are all in this together. We are all a family in adversity. So from this day on, that is how we will refer to ourselves. The Family.

"A great writer once wrote a book about three Musketeers. You might have heard of it or seen any of the many movies made. There is a line from that book and from those movies that applies to us, as well. One for all, and all for one. It sums up all that we are. A Family, one for all and all for one."

Carpenter gestured to encompass the Blocks, the moat, and the high wall. "Look around you. If we're a Family, what does that make our compound? From now on we will call it our Home. Start to think of it as that. Say it in your head. Get used to the idea. We are the Family and we live in the Home."

Someone spoke up. "That's all well and good, but what if we don't like some of our brothers or sisters?"

"What's unusual about that? Every Family has conflict. They work around it as we'll work around it. The important thing to keep in mind is that we can work anything out if we put our minds to it."

Carpenter waited so they could absorb all that he had said so far. Then he went on to the next phase. "Think of it. We have lived through the end of the world. All that we knew is gone. We are starting over, literally, and I would like to do some things differently from how they were done before."

"You're our leader," a woman declared.

"By default, yes. If you want to bestow that title on me, I accept it. But only under the condition that each of you accepts a title of your own."

"What do you mean?" This question came from a man on the far side.

"One of the problems that led to the hell we have lived through was the belief by some that they had the right to lord over everyone else. That they could decide what was right and wrong and how we should live our lives—or lose them, if need be—to keep them in power. Power mongers, they were, and they set themselves up above the rest of us.

"There will be none of that here. We are all equals. No one—and I emphasize this—no one has the right to set himself or herself above the rest of us. To prevent that, to keep anyone from getting a swelled head, all of us will be equally important. All of us will have titles of our own.

"So yes, call me the Leader if you want. But in a few days, when we begin to assign jobs based on your specific skills, each of you will have a title, too. Our doctor and nurses will be known as Healers. Our agricultural experts, those who will raise the crops that will sustain our Family over the long haul, will be called Tillers."

A man interrupted, "Is this really necessary? It strikes me as absurd."

"We are all equals, remember. There will be no artificial distinctions in the Home. No presidents, no senators, no kings or queens, and by extension, no commoners or average citizens. We are as the ancient Spartans were, peers. We will honor that equality with titles for each of us."

"I guess that makes sense."

Carpenter saw nods and smiles and forged on. "In the days to come I'll talk more about how I hope to see our Family organized, with your approval, of course.

"But there is one issue that won't wait, one we must deal with now for the safety of all." He paused. "You know about the incident in which our Home was invaded and we lost one of our own. You know that if not for the heroism of Mr. Slayne and Mr. Anderson, more lives would have been lost."

Out on the grass, Toril took Soren's hand in hers and gave him a tender squeeze. Magni grinned and patted his leg. Freya looked troubled.

"The attack has demonstrated a need. I blame myself for Mr. Richardson's death. I should have foreseen this contingency."

Diana Trevor spoke up. "Don't be so hard on yourself."

"I'm the Leader, aren't I? It's on my shoulders." Carpenter stopped. "But enough of my oversight. What we need is a small group whose sole purpose will be to defend the Home and protect the Family. I believe nine should do to start, but we'll add more as conditions warrant. In keeping with our new rule about titles, we'll call them Warriors."

Someone laughed. "Isn't that a tad pretentious?"

"No more so than calling me the Leader. And if you'll recall, the concept of the warrior has a long and noble history. The Spartans I've already alluded to. There were the samurai. The Minutemen. Special Forces. I could go on and on. Calling our fighters Warriors is more than appropriate."

No one disputed him.

"We're agreed? Good. I hereby choose Patrick Slayne to appoint the team of Warriors. With his military and security background, he is ideally suited to the task."

A woman raised her hand. "Is that all they'll do? Fight? What if he picks someone who is one of those Tillers you talked about? Who will fill the Tiller's shoes?"

"We'll make do as best we can. The Warriors are crucial to our survival. We can't just pick people and shove guns in their hands. They'll need to practice working together, so if and when the Home is attacked, they'll mesh as a team. If it develops that we don't need the Warriors to be on alert 24–7, then of course they can perform other duties as required. Does that answer your question?"

The woman nodded.

Carpenter glanced at Slayne. "Patrick, is there anything you'd like to say? Do you want to choose your people now or later?"

Slayne stood. "Brothers and sisters," he began, and grinned as he said it, "as head of security—pardon me—as a Warrior, I'll do my best to safeguard the life of every Family member. As we've already learned the hard way, the job calls for constant vigilance, and as our Leader pointed out, and Alf Richardson found out too late, it takes more than good intentions. For the Warriors to be effective, they must be true warriors in every sense of the word. They must be fighting machines."

"We're people, not machines," a woman said.

"Exactly. And because we *are* living, breathing beings, we

tend to make mistakes. We slip up. We don't pay attention when we should. We forget to do things." Slayne paused. "But I ask you to consider that mistakes cost lives. For our Warriors to make as few of them as is humanly possible, they must be carefully selected and just as carefully trained. We're not talking a few hours of target practice and hand-to-hand combat. No. For our Warriors to best serve and protect, for them to be the best they can be, they must train each and every day. I'll develop the program myself. We'll have them hone their skills to where they are the equal of any special ops unit in this country or any other."

A man coughed. "Aren't you asking a lot? I mean, I doubt many of us have combat experience."

"I'll find out exactly who does and who doesn't soon enough. But that's not all that important. The real issue is that those who become Warriors realize the depth of the commitment they must make."

"How will you select them?" a woman asked.

"I'll ask for volunteers. We can't ever force someone to put their life on the line against their will. Whoever applies must *want* to do it. They must be willing to fight and die for the Family and the Home. So any of you who feel in your heart that you can make that sacrifice, feel free to see me. After a sifting process, we'll pick those we deem best suited."

"We?"

"Our Leader, Diana Trevor and myself. Dr. Trevor, as some of you know, is an eminent psychologist and educator and has a say in all important Home matters."

A subdued ripple spread, prompting Kurt Carpenter to step forward and say, "Is something the matter?"

A burly man with arms as thick as tree trunks stood. "Sam Richter, Mr. Carpenter. I'm a blacksmith, remember?"

"Call me Kurt. A blacksmith and a weaponsmith, as I recall."

"I'd like to know if you meant what you said about us being equals and peers?"

"Of course I did."

"Then how is it that you and Dr. Trevor and Mr. Slayne, there, get to decide what's good for us and what isn't? How is it you pick the Warriors and we have no say?"

Carpenter went to answer, but Slayne put a hand on his arm.

"Mr. Richter, have you ever killed anyone?"

"Goodness, no, Mr. Slayne. I've never even been in a fight."

"I have. I've had to kill a number of times. Those who become Warriors will have to kill, too. It's the single most important ability, for want of a better word, a Warrior must have. Now I ask you, which of us is better able to judge whether someone has that ability? You, who by your own admission has never harmed a soul in your life? Or someone like me, the head of a worldwide security firm, a former navy SEAL and deputy sheriff?"

Richter grinned sheepishly. "I get your point."

"As for Professor Trevor," Carpenter said, "I've relied on her judgment a great deal in the formulation of my plans. She designed the tests you took to qualify to be here. Her psychological assessment of Warrior applicants will be invaluable."

He stopped and regarded the Family members a moment. "I know what some of you are thinking. That I've set myself up as your lord and master. But nothing could be further from the truth. I never make a decision without consulting those best able to give me advice. If the decision is important enough, if it affects our whole Family, then I give you my word that from this day on, I'll put it to a vote so everyone can have their say."

"That's reasonable," a woman declared.

A gust of wind hit Carpenter in the face. He glanced up. The sky seemed a darker shade of gray than it had been, and he would swear the gray was moving and rippling, almost as if it were alive.

A man waved a hand to get his attention. "Ed Batson, Kurt. Nurse. I have no interest in being a Warrior. I like to save lives, not destroy them. But I also like to think I'm practical, and it occurs to me that it might be wise to encourage everyone to wear or carry firearms, especially if we venture outside these walls."

The wind kept buffeting Carpenter. He gazed beyond the west wall and saw what he took to be rain in the distance. "You make a good point, Ed. Let's make it a rule, shall we, that no one leaves the Home unless they are armed or have someone with them who is."

An infant squealed and raised a tiny hand to the sky.

"When *will* we be able to go out?" an older man inquired. "The compound—sorry, our Home—has plenty of space, but I'd like to get out and about now and then."

"First things first. We must get the Home in order before we venture beyond the safety of its walls."

A small dark flake flitted out of the sky and landed on the grass.

"Is there anything any of you care to bring up?"

A woman with wavy red hair stood up. "Yes, there is. You can't expect us to stay in the bunkers forever. It's too crowded and there's hardly any privacy. Where will we live once it's safe to come out?"

Carpenter began to respond but stopped with his mouth half open as more flakes fell, some of them fluttering like butterflies. He reached out and a large flake landed on his palm. It reminded him of ash.

"What in the world?" someone blurted.

A woman turned her head to the sky and gasped. "Is that what I think it is?"

Carpenter glanced up, too, and icy fingers gripped his heart. The sky was filled with flakes. Not hundreds or thousands or hundreds of thousands but millions, descending in a quiet rain of potential death. For it wasn't ash, he realized; it was nuclear fallout.

"God in heaven."

Alpha Triad

Patrick Slayne instantly assumed command. "Everyone into their assigned bunkers! On your feet! Do it quick but do it orderly! Move, people! *Move!*" He touched Carpenter, who was staring upward as if mesmerized. "That means you, too, Kurt. Get in C Block."

Carpenter tore his gaze from the deluge. He blinked and said, "The Family first."

"A lot of us are expendable. You're not." Slayne motioned to Diana Trevor. "Get him in there. Push him if he won't walk."

Diana nodded and took hold of Carpenter's wrist. "He's right. Your safety is paramount."

The Family made an orderly dash for sanctuary as more and more flakes fluttered down, a dark snowfall, growing thicker and darker, moment by moment.

Slayne was furious with himself. He should have posted lookouts with orders to keep a watch on the sky as well as beyond the walls. His lapse might cost lives.

By now the ground was completely covered. Visibility was limited to twenty feet, at best.

"Faster!" Slayne shouted. "As fast as you can!" He moved among them, hastening them along. "Hold hands and call out if you lose your way!"

To their credit, no one panicked. Mothers clasped children and fathers shielded their young ones with their own bodies.

Slayne was the last to make for the Blocks. By then visibility was down to five feet. Cupping his hands, he bellowed, "Have someone standing next to each Block yell so the others can get their bearings." Almost immediately, some of those who had already reached the bunkers began calling out.

Slayne reached C Block. But he didn't go in. He stood just outside, the fallout so thick he could barely see his hand at arm's length, and listened to the shouting until it stopped. Then, shaking himself and brushing off flakes, he entered and nodded at two men waiting to shut the door. He made straight for the Com Center and contacted each of the other Blocks.

Everyone was accounted for.

A man ran up with a Geiger counter. "I've been checking like you said we always should when we come back in. The needle is jumping."

Slayne confirmed it for himself. The fallout read high but not so high as to be life-threatening, except for a few hot particles. He barked commands. Everyone was to strip off the clothes they had worn outside and the clothes were to be piled in a corner of the laundry. Cleanup details were to go from room to room, sweeping up ash. Hot particles were to be isolated and disposed of.

Slayne relayed his instructions to the other Blocks. He could only hope no one came down with radiation sickness. When he had done all he could, he went in search of Carpenter and found him seated at his desk looking distraught. "It could have been worse," he concluded.

"A lot worse," Carpenter agreed. "I didn't react fast enough. You did, though. You assumed charge quickly and efficiently."

Slayne shrugged. "It's my job."

Carpenter thoughtfully drummed his fingers on his desk. "Another lesson learned. From here on out, in times of emergency you're to assume charge of the Family."

"Don't go overboard."

"I'm not, Patrick. In fact, I intend to ask for a vote of general approval so that in the future, whenever the Home is threatened, the Warriors will take over until the crisis has passed."

Diana Trevor came in. She had changed into a light blue blouse and jeans. "I think that went well, all things considered."

Slayne frowned. "We were caught napping. But I'll be damned if I'll let that happen again."

"I guess I should have listened to that girl. Maybe it wouldn't have happened." Diana sank into a chair.

"What girl? What are you talking about?

"Megan Franchone. She's, what, fifteen? This morning I was talking to her family at breakfast and the mother mentioned Megan had a dream last night that something terrible would happen today. I told her dreams like that are perfectly ordinary."

"I wonder," Carpenter said. "Have the mother and the girl come see me later. I'd like to find out if she has dreams like that often."

"Oh, she does. The mother tried to convince me that

Megan is some kind of psychic. Which is perfectly ridiculous."

"Is it?" Carpenter leaned back. "I read an article on it once in a Fortean magazine. Empaths, such people are called."

"Kurt, please."

"I know, I know. But there have been documented cases that can't be explained."

"I'm surprised at you. Usually you take a more rational approach."

"I try to leave myself open to all possibilities," Carpenter said. "I had a college instructor who used to say that the only thing that keeps us from solving the challenges we face is a closed mind."

Slayne changed the subject. "I'm going to get on the horn and announce that anyone interested in being a Warrior should contact me. I'll conduct personal interviews later, after the fallout stops and we know it's safe."

"I wonder how many will apply?"

Fourteen men and women were interested. Slayne weeded out those whose hearts were in the right place but who lacked the most essential attribute for the job. As he explained it to one of the volunteers, "Anyone can learn to shoot. Anyone can learn to fight. But that's not enough. True Warriors must have a certain mindset. They must be devoted to combat. They must live it, eat it, breathe it. They must learn to live on the cusp of death. The deaths they cause, and their own."

The candidate asked for Slayne to elaborate.

"When all is said and done, the essence of being a Warrior is death dealing. If a person isn't comfortable as a death dealer, they lack the most essential quality a Warrior needs. So far there are only two Family members who

I can say with complete confidence have that quality, and one of them is me."

"Who is the other one?"

Soren Anderson strode over to a corner table in the cafeteria, set Mjolnir down, and took a seat across from the man who was eating. "Do you mind if we talk?"

"Not at all." Sam Richter paused with a piece of meatloaf halfway to his mouth and stared at the hammer. "So that's what you used? A mallet against rifles. You have guts." He bit the meatloaf off the fork and chewed. "Word is that you've been selected to be a Warrior. Congratulations."

"Thank you. That's why I'm here. Mr. Carpenter says you're the Family Armorer."

Richter chuckled. "Him and his titles. I'm a blacksmith, Mr. Anderson. Before that I had a gun shop for a few years. I can take a gun apart and put it back together again."

"I'm not here about a gun." Soren placed a big hand on Mjolnir. "I'm here about this."

Richater put down his fork and picked up a glass of water. "I'm not sure I understand."

"The Warriors are required to carry at least two guns. One must be a rifle or a shotgun or a submachine gun. The other must be a sidearm. I don't want a sidearm. I want to use Mjolnir."

"I still don't understand."

"Can you turn Mjolnir into a gun? Can you rig it so I can shoot a bullet out the handle?"

Sam Richter reached across the table to lift the hammer using one hand. "Dear lord." He used both hands. "How can you swing this thing? It must weigh fifty pounds."

"To me it is a feather."

"Maybe you should listen to Slayne."

"But I want Mjolnir. All I need is to find a way to give it more range and he'll let me use it. I'm sure."

Richter examined the hammer closely. He ran his fingers over the runes and thumped the head and then the handle. "Mr. Anderson, this thing is solid. A gun requires parts to operate. Where would I put them?"

"I was thinking the handle."

Richter turned the hammer upside down and placed it on the table with its handle sticking up. "What kind of wood is this? Whatever it is, it's as hard as rock. I could try to core it out, but even then I'm not sure I could fit a trigger mechanism inside."

Soren didn't hide his disappointment. "There must be something. Maybe it could fire a shotgun shell if you put in a firing pin and I pound it a certain way."

"The pounding might break the pin. And it would only work at extremely close range." Richter shook his head. "I'm sorry. I truly am. But I don't see how I can be of help."

"I was afraid of that." Soren sadly picked up Mjolnir and held it high. "If only I could be like the son of Odin and call down the thunder and lightning."

About to resume eating, Richter looked at him and then at the hammer. "Lightning, you say?"

"Yes. Surely you've read of Thor's exploits?"

"Can't say as I have, no. But you've just given me an idea. Ever used an electroshock weapon like a Taser or one of those new Voltz? I sold them back when I had my gun shop."

Soren shook his head. The only time he had ever seen them was on television and in the movies.

"They made great strides in miniaturization right before this damn war. The Voltz looked like a pen, but it packed quite a wallop. Up to two million volts, if I remember correctly."

"What are you suggesting?"

Richter came around the table and examined the hammer more closely. "Would you trust me to replace this handle? Say, with a titanium alloy, hollowed out so I can fit it with those new solarium capacitors and a selector switch? All insulated, of course, so you only fry those you're fighting and not yourself."

"I'll be able to stun people?" Soren liked the idea, but it wasn't what he had had in mind and certainly wouldn't convince Slayne to let him use Mjolnir.

"Oh, I think we can do better than that." Richter circled the handle with two fingers, gauging how thick it was. "There's this young man named Allan Timm. He's the Assistant Armorer, as Carpenter calls him. Allan is a gun nut, but he's also quite good at electronics. With his help we should be able to outdo the commercial models."

"How would it work, exactly?" Soren asked. "I'd shoot little darts out of the handle?" Even that didn't appeal to him.

"Oh, no, Mr. Anderson. Didn't you ever read *Popular Mechanics*? The latest versions use the air as a conductor."

Soren drummed the table in mild impatience. "Spell it out for me, Mr. Richter. What *exactly* will I be able to do?"

The Armorer smiled. "You'll be able to shoot lightning bolts."

A tingle ran from the nape of Soren's neck to the base of his spine. He said, almost breathlessly, "You're kidding me."

"Not at all." Richter scratched his chin. "Let's see. If I make the new handle longer, we can rig it so you can trigger a discharge several times without recharging. I should guess it would give you a range of twenty or thirty feet."

"Dear Odin."

Richter was absorbed in the challenge. "As added protection we should come up with special gloves. Rubber would work. Maybe even a whole suit. Like one of those wet suits that divers wear." He paused. "I wonder if Carpenter has one stockpiled somewhere?"

Images danced in Soren's head. He grabbed the Armorer's hand and enthusiastically pumped it. "If you can do this, Mr. Richter, I'll be forever in your debt."

"Don't get excited yet. I have to run it past Allan. He's the one who can make it work. Why don't you bring your hammer by my workshop in an hour or so for him to look at?"

"I'll be there." Soren grabbed Mjolnir and hurried out to break the news to Toril. In his excitement he nearly collided with someone coming the other way. "Oh. Sorry, Mr. Carpenter. I didn't see you."

Kurt Carpenter was consulting a digital clipboard. "Mmmm?" he said absently, and looked up. "Mr. Anderson. How are you? I want to personally thank you for volunteering to be a Warrior. Patrick tells me you're one of his most promising recruits."

That reminded Soren of something. "Did he talk to you about my code name?"

"Your what?"

Soren explained that Slayne had insisted each of the Warriors use a code name.

"He says they are common, that Special Forces use them when on combat ops, as he calls it." Soren hesitated, then came out with it: "But when I told him the name I want to use, he called it silly. Inappropriate, was his exact word."

"What do you want to be called?"

"Thor."

Carpenter coughed, then said, "It's rather unusual."

"I just don't want anyone to forget," Soren said.

"Forget what?"

"The God of Thunder." Soren let out his passion. "Think about it, sir. The world has pretty much come to an end. All those cities destroyed. All those millions and millions killed. Civilization has to start over. But without electricity and with all the schools closed and a lot of the libraries destroyed, who will remember the things of the past? Who will remember Thor? Or those Spartans you were talking about? Or anything having to do with history? It will all be forgotten."

Kurt Carpenter gave a start. "I hadn't thought of that." He gnawed his lower lip. "Mr. Anderson, you've given me an inspiration. I must think on it more, but I thank you." He started to go on by.

"Wait. What about my code name?"

Carpenter smiled. "From this moment on we'll call you Thor."

First Run

Two weeks of intense training was all they had. Slayne would have liked to spend longer, but Carpenter insisted they must find out what happened to the SEAL. "I can't stress how important it will be to those who come after us."

The entire Family saw them off.

Carpenter climbed to the rampart above the moat and raised his arms to get everyone's attention. "This is a momentous day. Our first foray into the devastated world. We have no idea what our Warriors will find, but it's safe to say their travels will not be without peril. We wish them Godspeed."

From all sides came cheers and waves.

Slayne wheeled the Hunster over the drawbridge. "This is our first combat op as a team, and it's bound to be rough. We haven't had nearly enough time to work together. Follow my lead and keep your headsets on at all times and we should make it back alive and in one piece. Any questions?"

"What was it Kurt Carpenter said we were to call ourselves?" Montoya asked.

Slayne chuckled. "Alpha Triad. I wanted it to be Alpha Team or even the A-Team but he thought Alpha Triad had a ring to it. You know how he is."

At the outset they made good time.

Patrick Slayne did most of the driving. He let Soren Anderson and Robert Montoya spell him, but only for a few hours when he needed sleep so badly he couldn't keep his eyes open. They took 59 to 11 and followed 11 west to Interstate 29.

Full gas cans in a rack at the rear of the Hunster ensured they wouldn't want for fuel.

For the longest while the roads were empty of traffic. East of the turn to Drayton they spotted a jeep in the distance, but apparently whoever was in it spotted them and wasn't anxious to make their acquaintance. The jeep wheeled off the road and disappeared into shadowed woodland.

Here and there were swathes of fallout. In some areas it was thicker than in others. The Geiger counter often spiked, but Slayne assured them that they were safe so long as they stayed in the Hunster and kept on the move.

They turned south on 29. Almost immediately they came across abandoned vehicles and wrecks.

Between Oakwood and Warsaw they crested a low hill and Slayne slammed on the brakes. The interstate was completely blocked by a row of wrecked vehicles placed hood to trunk.

"Someone put them there on purpose." Soren stated the obvious.

In the back, Robert Montoya leaned between the front seats. "Should we turn around and go to the last exit?"

"And waste an hour?" Slayne shook his head and put his

foot to the gas pedal. He held his finger over the red button on the dash. "If it's what I think it is, they're in for a surprise."

"They?" Soren said.

No sooner was the question out of his mouth than men with rifles and handguns rose up from behind the roadblock. A tall man climbed onto the roof of a car and raised a megaphone to his mouth.

"You there! Stop and get out with your hands in the air! We won't tell you twice!"

"Like hell." Slayne pressed the red button.

The Hunster shook, and a split second later the ground in front of the car on which the man was standing erupted in a shower of asphalt and dirt. The man and his companions scattered.

Slayne tramped harder on the gas and the Hunster picked up speed. He engaged the battering ram. "Make sure you're strapped in and hold on tight."

Lead spanged off the vehicle's body and windshield. None of it had an appreciable effect, thanks to the armor plating and bulletproof glass.

Slayne roared through the opening he had made, doing sixty miles an hour.

On both sides men cut loose with a fierce vengeance, but they were soon left in the Hunster's dust. Slayne chuckled. "I love this baby. She's everything I'd hoped she would be." He glanced at the rearview mirror to see if they were being chased; they weren't.

Soren asked a question that had been preying on him. "If this one is so great, what do we need the other one for?"

"The SEAL? Kurt spent millions developing it. The SEAL has capabilities that even the Hunster doesn't. And he has very specific plans for how it will be used. Important plans."

"They must be important to risk your baby and three Warriors," Robert Montoya said. He was dressed in camouflage fatigues and combat boots. In a flapped holster on his right hip was a Colt Commander .45, while propped on the seat beside him was a Jati-Matic out of Finland, one of the various foreign firearms Slayne had talked Carpenter into adding to the Armory.

"Risk comes with the territory," Slayne reminded him. "You knew that when you took Kurt's new Warrior oath." Slayne wore his dark blue trench coat over the same business suit he had worn the day he retrieved Deepak Kapur in New York City. In twin shoulder holsters nestled twin Mark 23s, the compact models commissioned by the U.S. Special Operations Command but never mass-produced. In a pack around his waist he had spare magazines, two silencers, and a laser spot projector.

"If the SEAL is that important," Soren broke in, "why did Carpenter only send the three of us? Why not four Warriors? Or even five?"

"Why not all nine?" Slayne rejoined. "That way there wouldn't be anyone left to protect the Home." He switched on the map display. "Only having three in each unit was my idea. As I told Kurt, there's always an extra if a man goes down."

Soren gazed out the window and saw his reflection. Black neoprene fit as snugly as skin. So did the neoprene boots and gloves. He looked ready to go scuba diving, save for the power belt. Under lightweight and durable black synthetic chain mail was the computerized circuitry that enabled him to recharge Mjolnir. All he had to do was fit the handle into a clamp in the center, which connected to positive and negative electrodes, and throw a switch. An LCD display showed the recharge rate. As a protective measure, the belt was insulated so he wouldn't be accidentally jolted.

"What I'd like to know," Montoya said, "is how we can be sure the SEAL is even there?"

"We can't."

"Then this whole trip might be a wild goose chase."

"If it will make you feel any better, think of it as a practice run. We're the first Warriors, the first Family members ever, to travel outside the walls. What we find will determine Family policy for years to come."

"I miss my family," Soren said. He could not stop thinking about Toril, Freya, and Magni.

"Remember what I've taught you and you'll see them again," Slayne said. "Rely on your shotgun more than that hammer and you'll live longer."

Soren offered no reply. He had already made up his mind about which weapon he would use the most.

The winds hit them near Spiritwood.

They had pulled off the road to switch drivers and stretch their legs. Soren took Mjolnir, as was his habit.

The sky was gray, as usual. Flakes fell but not in any great number. The top of a nearby tree shook, then stopped.

Soren moved to the side of the road, searching for tracks or any other sign of life. A strong wind buffeted him but he ignored it.

"I don't like the looks of that," Robert Montoya said.

To the west, the gray was acting strangely. Instead of its usual flat appearance there were swirls and eddies, as there would be in agitated water.

"Odd," Soren remarked.

The strongest gust yet made the grass bend nearly in half.

"Into the Hunster," Slayne directed. He didn't like the looks of it, either. He climbed into the driver's seat.

Soren reluctantly turned. He would have liked a few more minutes to walk around and stretch his cramped muscles.

He had taken another step when suddenly a wall of wind slammed into him and knocked him sideways. He lost his balance and nearly fell.

As quickly as it had struck, the wind died.

Montoya had been thrown against the Hunster so hard, he dropped the Jati-Matic. "Where did that come from?"

"Get in," Slayne said.

Soren looked up. A peculiar keening filled the air, like the distant wail of banshees, growing louder by the second. "Do you hear that?"

"I said to get in. Now."

The urgency in Slayne's tone prompted Soren to move. "I thought I was driving."

Slayne gestured toward the passenger seat. He turned the ignition and was in gear when Soren climbed in. Without delay he headed down the highway, glancing right and left. "I remember a scientist who theorized on the effects of an all-out nuclear war. One of them was what he called nuclear winds."

"Never heard of it," Montoya said.

"You should have read more science magazines and less science fiction, Ricco," Slayne said, using Montoya's code name instead of his real name. He had been trying to get them to do the same. "Listen." He lowered his window several inches.

The keening was now a screech.

Montoya covered his ears. "I don't like the sound of that, Solo." He emphasized Slayne's own code name.

Soren liked it. The wind and the howling made him think of a thunderstorm.

Since he was a child he'd loved storms as other boys loved baseball or video games or cars. Maybe that was part of the reason he later took to Thor so avidly. The thunder god was lord of the storm and embodied all that Soren most admired in nature and in life.

Slayne slowed. He had spotted a field and what appeared to be a gully or a wash. Spinning the steering wheel, he floored it.

The screech had become a shriek. The whole sky seemed to be moving with incredible speed.

Slayne prayed they had enough time. The Hunster bounced over ruts and plowed through weeds, and then they were at the top of the gully. A glance told him it was wide enough and deep enough, and he plunged on down without braking.

For a few harrowing heartbeats the Hunster canted and threatened to roll, but it leveled at the bottom. He turned the engine off.

Above them, the very heavens screamed.

"What do you expect will happen?" Robert Montoya asked.

The answer came in the form of a windstorm to end all windstorms.

Its roar was fit to burst the eardrums. Dust rose in a thick cloud. The Hunster shook so violently, it was a wonder it wasn't blown onto its side.

Montoya pressed his face to his window. "*Madre de dios*. How long will this last?"

"No telling."

"If this were to hit the Home when people were outside . . ." Montoya didn't finish.

Soren settled back, Mjolnir in his lap. He ran his fingers over the new metal handle, admiring how well Richter had duplicated the runes on the original. Only now each rune was a stud that controlled a specific function. He couldn't wait to put the hammer to the test in actual battle.

Soren turned to Montoya. Since they had nothing else to do until the wind stopped, he thought it time he learned more about his fellow Warrior. "Where are you from, if you don't mind my asking?"

"I was born and raised in San Diego." Montoya's features clouded. "My *madre*, my *padre*, my sisters, my brothers, they're all gone."

"You still have your wife."

"*Si*. If not for Theresa, I don't know what I would do. She's my anchor and my life."

For the first time since they met, Soren felt a fledgling bond. Montoya was housed in E Block, and they had only been thrust together a week ago to prepare for the SEAL run, as Carpenter liked to refer to it. "What did you do before the war? I was in construction."

Montoya chuckled. "I was in the army. Stationed at Fort Riley. When the task force was destroyed, I phoned Theresa and had her fly to Denver. I met her there and we flew on to Minnesota."

"They let you leave the base?" Soren recalled hearing on the radio that all military leaves had been canceled.

"I'm AWOL," Montoya said quietly.

"You did what you had to do to get your wife to safety," Slayne interjected. "If you hadn't left when you did, you'd have been stranded when all the aircraft were grounded."

Soren discovered that Montoya had been in the First Infantry Division and was rated a marksman. "It will be great to work together."

"Or die together."

"Stow that kind of talk," Slayne growled. "You're a Warrior now, mister, and Warriors don't die without my permission."

Soren and Montoya both laughed, and were promptly

sobered by a blast of wind that shook the Hunster down to its axles.

The minutes crawled. Half an hour became an hour and the hour became two. All around them, cyclonic winds raged.

At one point Slayne shifted in his seat to say, "Remember what I told you back at the Home. In the field, use your code names, not your real names. Robert, you should be used to stealth ops. Soren, you were a civilian, so it might help if you started using our code names all the time so it comes naturally in combat."

"Wait." Soren had to absorb this. "You *want* me to think of myself as Thor?"

"Do you have a problem with that?"

Shaking with silent mirth, Soren shook his head. "No, Mr. Slayne, no problem at all."

"What did I just tell you?"

"Oh, sorry. No, Solo, I don't."

Twenty minutes later, as abruptly as the winds had started, they died. In the sudden stillness Slayne rolled down his window. Quiet reigned. The gray sky once again moved at a snail's pace. He turned the Hunster over and drove out of the gully.

Every last vestige of vegetation for miles around had been destroyed. The grass and weeds had been scoured from the earth. Most of the trees were down.

Not one had any leaves left, or much bark.

"Let's hope we don't run into that again." Slayne drove to the road and continued west.

They took 200 to State Highway 83 and crossed the Missouri River at Washburn. Half a dozen times they spotted other people but always at a distance.

"Is it me, or is everyone avoiding the roads?" Montoya mentioned.

They saw deer. They saw a few birds. They braked for a black bear that crossed in front of them, but it paid them no mind. A lot of its fur was missing and it kept twitching and jerking as it walked.

Avoiding cities and towns, they made it across North Dakota and into Montana. Slayne decided to dare Interstate 94 in the belief that they would make better time. For a while, they did. Then, northeast of Miles City, they crested a low rise and beheld a sight that caused Slayne to stomp on the brake to bring the Hunster to a stop.

A man lay on his back in the middle of the highway. He was surrounded by people—and they were eating him.

A Taste of Things to Come

Soren Anderson reeled. He kept thinking that he couldn't be seeing what he thought he was seeing.

There were about twenty of them. Their clothes were filthy and torn and some were in tatters. The people were filthy, too. But it wasn't the filth that shocked Soren. It was the sores or lesions that spotted their skin, boiling festers that oozed green pus.

Their eyes, when they raised their heads and stared dumbly at the Hunster, were dull and glazed and so bloodshot they were pits of red. Saliva oozed from their open mouths in steady streams of drool.

"Dear Odin," Soren breathed. "What's wrong with them?"

"A chemical weapon, maybe," Slayne said. "Or one of the new bio bugs."

As CEO of Tekco he had heard rumors of things like this, and worse.

Montoya gaped in disgust. "But why are they *eating* him? Why not hunt or find canned food?"

The things went back to their feeding. One gnawed on an intestine. Another chewed on a dripping chunk of leg.

"They're ignoring us," Montoya said. "Go around them. Let's get out of here."

Slayne nodded, but as he went to press the gas, the back door opened. "Thor? What in hell are you doing?"

"This is an abomination. It must not be." Soren walked around to the front of the Hunster, Mjolnir at his side. He remembered what the Family Armorer had told him. The hammer could be set to Arc or Bolt. In addition there were four power settings. The lowest was a million volts, and it went up in million-volt increments from here. At four million, the highest, the blast drained the hammer completely and Mjolnir couldn't be used again until he recharged it using the power belt. But he wouldn't need that much now. He pressed the appropriate rune, setting the hammer to Arc and one million volts. He raised Mjolnir. "I am Thor. I command you to stop."

The festering horrors fixed their red eyes on him. They were eerily silent.

Then those on their knees rose, and they all came toward him at once, moving with a peculiar shambling gait, their mouths opening and closing as if they were gulping for air.

Soren's skin crawled, but he held his ground. He pressed the rune to fire.

Mjolnir jumped in Soren's hands. The head glowed bright and hummed.

From the weapon lanced crackling lightning bolts that arced and leaped at the advancing monstrosities, striking them in the head, face, and chest. Half died on their feet, writhing and contorting and jerking like puppets on invisible strings. They didn't scream. They didn't cry out. Those still standing closed in and Soren unleashed a second blast.

Bodies dropped, thud after thud.

"Sweet Odin," Soren breathed. He had practiced with Mjolnir but not on living foes. Only two were still alive, and they came for him, their hands outstretched. Revulsion swept through him. He crushed the skull of the first and reduced the face of the second to splintered pulp.

Soren moved among them, making sure. Some had burn marks. Some were giving off smoke. He swallowed and looked at Mjolnir, felt the familiar tingle down his spine. "So much power," he said in awe.

"What in hell did you think you were doing?" Slayne and Montoya had come out of the Hunster, and Slayne wasn't happy. "You could have been killed."

"I couldn't just sit there. I had to do something."

"They were no threat to us. We could have gone on by. Get it through your head that you can't go taking needless risks."

"I did what the son of Odin would do."

Slayne held his temper. "Just because we call you Thor doesn't *make* you Thor. Damn it, Anderson. You have a responsibility to the Family. You can't go throwing your life away on a whim."

"I do what I must," Soren insisted.

Montoya stared at Mjolnir. "I've never seen anything like it," he said in awe. "I want one of those."

Soren reverently held the hammer to his chest. "Mjolnir is the only one of its kind."

"How does it work?"

"I don't understand all the science," Soren admitted. Richter and Allan had told him that the higher the power setting, the higher the current it induced, and that it was the current more than the volts that killed. But then they had also told him that it was the volts that could blast limbs from bodies.

Slayne scanned the bleak landscape. "Get in. There might be more of those monstrosities around."

They gave Billings a wide berth. Later, twice, they spied antelope, but always at a distance. Once they came upon a dog moving stiffly at the side of the highway. Montoya wanted to stop until he saw that most of its hair was gone and it was covered with sores.

Between Bozeman and Butte, as they crossed a barren flat, Slayne braked and got out the binoculars.

"What do you see?" Montoya asked.

Slayne pointed. "You tell me, Ricco."

To the north was a cloud. Not in the sky, but on the ground. It was green, bright green, so bright it seemed to glow, and it was *moving*, crawling across the ground as if endowed with a will of its own.

"What *is* that?"

Slayne didn't know. It wasn't much bigger than the Hunster and was heading east, away from them. He resumed driving and commented, "Welcome to our warped new world."

Roadblocks had been set up around Missoula. A National Guard unit, judging by their uniforms and equipment. Slayne spied them from half a mile out and decided to go around.

The Bitterroot Mountains of eastern Idaho were a pristine wonder. Except for areas of scattered fallout, the Bitterroots were as they had always been. Or so Slayne thought until it occurred to him that there should be more signs of animal life.

They were east of Wallace—and only twenty miles from

Smelterville—when they rounded a curve and a crudely made billboard warned Checkpoint Ahead.

Slayne quickly stopped. Several hundred yards down the highway were concrete barriers topped by barbed wire. Heavily armed men moved about behind the barricade. They weren't in uniform.

"What do we have here?" Montoya wondered.

"To the right of the roadblock is a sign." Slayne gave him the binoculars. "It explains a lot."

Montoya read the sign out loud. "WARNING. YOU ARE ABOUT TO ENTER THE FREE ARYAN NATION. WEAPONS ARE SUBJECT TO SEIZURE. NO DRUGS OR ALCOHOL ARE ALLOWED BEYOND THIS POINT."

"Read the fine print at the bottom."

"NO PERSONS OF COLOR ADMITTED." Montoya lowered the binoculars. "You've got to be kidding me."

"Northern Idaho was an Aryan stronghold before the war. From here to the Washington border must be their territory now." Slayne pondered for a few moments. "A lot of them were survivalists. They mobilized at the outset of the war and I would guess that it was Ben Thomas's bad luck to run into them."

"Do you think they killed him?"

"Who knows? The important question is what have they done with the SEAL? We're not leaving without it."

Montoya nodded toward the barrier. "Before we can leave we have to get in. And I'll be damned if they're confiscating *my* weapons."

Slayne shifted into reverse. "They don't appear to have noticed us yet."

He backed around the curve and made a U-turn. "Thor, you're being unusually quiet. What's going on in that crazy Norse head of yours?"

"A man is more important than a machine."

The forest bordering the highway was thick, the undergrowth heavy, but Slayne managed to find a rutted track that suited his purpose. He went far enough to ensure the Hunster couldn't be seen from the road, then stopped. Climbing out, he slid his blue trench coat from over the back of his seat and shrugged into it.

"A little warm for that, isn't it?" Montoya said.

"I like to sweat." Slayne hadn't told anyone the real reason he always wore it. The trench coat was custom-constructed to his specifications. Woven from the newest Kevlar weave, it was so soft and pliable a person would swear it was cotton or wool. Yet it was impervious to small-arms fire.

Montoya went to the rear of the Hunster and swung its back door up. He donned a backpack and a helmet, then passed wafer-thin headsets to Slayne and Anderson. He didn't need one; his helmet came with an internal com link. He switched it on and tweaked the gain. "Testing. Testing. Are you picking up?"

"Clear as can be," Slayne said.

Soren adjusted the clip around his ear and nodded. "I hear you."

Slayne reached in and brought out the MP5. "Listen up. We go in, we find the SEAL if it's there, and we get out. We avoid contact as much as possible. We don't want a firefight if we can help it."

"What about Ben Thomas?" Soren wanted to know.

"More than likely he's dead by now. We have to focus on getting the SEAL back now."

Soren frowned.

Slayne slung the MP5 over his shoulder. "From here on out only use code names. When I say Alpha Triad, it means both of you." He headed back down the track toward the highway. "Single file," he snapped into his mouthpiece. "Ten-yard intervals. Ricco, after me. Thor, you bring up the rear. Stay frosty."

"Yes, sir," Montoya said.

"Thor?" Slayne prompted when there was no response from him.

"I hear you."

"Then say you do. We've been through all this, Anderson. Strict military procedure, remember?"

"I'm not really a soldier."

"You better start thinking like one. You're a *Warrior*, damn it. Get that through your thick Norwegian head. Our lives are on the line here. I don't know about you but I want to make it back to the Home."

"As do I. I have a lovely wife and two fine children. Don't worry. As the son of Odin does his duty, I'll do mine."

"The who?"

"The real Thor. The defender of Asgard and protector of Midgard. The bringer of the storm, the lord of the thunder and lightning."

"Spare me the mythological garbage and concentrate on the mission."

"As you wish."

When they reached the highway they crossed to the other side and paralleled it until they neared the barricade. Flattening, they crawled within earshot.

Slayne counted nine Aryans. Two had SMGs, the rest high-powered rifles.

Several were playing cards. One man was writing on a sheet of paper. No one was paying much attention to the highway. They were sloppy, this bunch. He could drop half of them before they knew what hit them, but he didn't. He was about to crawl on when a short bundle of sinew with a neatly trimmed goatee said something that perked his interest.

"When do you think Croft will give the word to move on Spokane?"

"Your guess is as good as mine," another Aryan answered. "Hardin thinks it will be a couple of weeks yet. The scouts haven't come back and we don't want to go up against more than we can handle."

"The Aryan Nation can handle anything."

Slayne whispered into his headset, "Alpha Triad, on me." He continued crawling. Once it was safe, he rose into a crouch. "We have a long way to go yet. We'll double time a few miles."

"Lead the way, Solo," Montoya said.

"Thor? Acknowledge, damn it."

"As he said, lead the way. The son of Odin will not fail you."

Slayne didn't like the sound of that. Anderson was taking the whole Thor business much too literally. But now wasn't the time or place to bring it up. Slayne began to jog.

The gray sky cast the woods in somber shadow. Normally the wilds were alive with the warbling of birds and the chittering of squirrels but it was graveyard quiet save for the rustling of the wind.

Slayne relied on a GPS unit. From a slope south of Wallace they surveyed the town. Save for a lot of armed men—and women—it could have been any town in prewar America.

A flag flew above a church. The flag's background was blue and red, with a gold crown atop a sword and what looked to be a horizontal Z through the middle.

"What does that stand for?" Montoya wondered.

"You'd have to ask them," Slayne said. "Not that they would answer you. To them you're one of the mud people."

"The what?"

"Anyone who isn't white. As a Hispanic you'd rate above a black but below a Jew."

"I sure would like to waste a few of these bigots."

The next town was Osburn. An Aryan flag flew over a church there, too. Kellogg, farther on, had half a dozen flags, but then it was twice the size of Osburn. The Warriors saw children playing and laughing, and heard someone singing.

On a normal day the sun would have been blazing the western horizon red, orange, and yellow when the Warriors reached a rise above Smelterville, but on this day there was only the perpetually gray sky. Slayne raked the town from end to end with the binoculars. He spotted four tractor-trailer rigs. One was parked on the main street. Two others were in residential areas. The last one, the one that interested him the most, was in the lot of a run-down factory.

"Gentlemen, take a gander." He passed the binoculars to Montoya and pointed.

"How do you want to handle this?"

"We separate and go in from different directions. Stay in touch at all times. Remember not to engage hostiles unless you absolutely have to. Understood, Ricco?"

Montoya grinned. "I'm good to go, Solo."

"And you, Thor?"

"I and Mjolnir are at your disposal."

"Then let's do this."

Compared to the other towns, Smelterville was strangely quiet. It bothered Slayne. It was always the unforeseen that sent a combat op south. On the plus side, the few people on the streets were moving about in a leisurely fashion, and he saw no evidence of checkpoints or any Aryan militia.

Slayne came to the edge of the forest. Beyond lay a side street lined by frame homes. "Solo is in position."

"Almost to mine," Montoya said.

Thor said nothing.

Slayne was beginning to have his doubts about the man. Anderson had performed admirably during the firefight at the Home, but he had been acting erratically ever since the Armorer had modified his hammer. Slayne wasn't a psychologist like Professor Trevor, but Anderson was acting more and more as if he thought he was the real Thor, and that was just plain psycho.

"This is Ricco. I'm in position."

"The son of Odin is where he should be."

"Use your code name from now on," Slayne said brusquely. He moved out from the trees. "All right, Alpha Triad. Converge on the truck. Low profile is the key phrase here."

Slayne's idea of a low profile was to sling the MP5 over his shoulder and stroll along as if he belonged there. An old lady sat in a rocking chair on a porch, knitting. He nodded at her and she nodded back.

From somewhere in the distance Slayne thought he heard subdued voices.

Montoya was supposed to come in from the east, Anderson from the west, and Slayne was approaching from the south. He had figured that one stranger, walking alone, was less likely to stand out and draw attention than three strangers together.

On the next street some boys were throwing a football. Slayne walked close to the curb. One or two glanced at him and went right back to their game. He was almost to the end of the block when a small dog came out of a yard and yipped at his heels. A woman called, "Here, Sweetiepie!" and the mutt scampered off.

The factory was set well back. Its parking lot had enough parking spaces to accommodate a hundred cars. The sign out front was faded. Slayne guessed that the place had closed years if not decades ago. A chain-link fence surrounded the lot but the gate was open and hanging lopsided.

The muffled voices grew louder.

As Slayne entered the parking lot, he realized why; the voices were coming from inside the factory. Some kind of meeting was going on. He made for the semi. "Alpha Triad, report."

"This is Ricco. Almost there."

"This is Thor. The same."

"Hold your positions once you reach the target," Slayne reminded them. They were to cover him from the perimeter and be ready to render aid if he needed it.

The truck was a regal mechanical beast with the words Semper Fi painted on the doors. The dust that covered it showed it had not seen recent use.

Slayne walked the length of the trailer. He looked around to verify no one was watching. Gripping the handle, he wrenched on the rear door. To his surprise, it opened right up. And there it was: the SEAL. He was surprised the Aryans hadn't tried to get it out. But maybe they had tried, and couldn't do it. The locks were ingeniously designed to thwart even the best lock pick, and the windows and body were proof against anything short of a bazooka. "It's here," he announced. "Baby is here."

"Roger that, Solo."

"I'll see if I can get the truck started. Hold your positions."

"Will do."

Slayne closed the door and hurried to the cab. The door was unlocked. He climbed in but left the door open. The key wasn't in the ignition, as he'd hoped it might be.

He checked behind the visors, in the glove compartment, and under the seat.

He debated trying to hotwire the truck.

"What the dickens are you doing in there, mister?"

The Aryan was short and stocky with close-cropped hair and a beard streaked with tobacco stains. He held a shotgun in his left hand, muzzle pointed at the ground.

"Looking for the key," Slayne said. "You wouldn't happen to have it, would you?"

"What? No. I'd guess Mr. Croft or Hardin has it. Mr.

Croft seems to think that van in the back is special. He gave orders that no one is to go near it without his say so."

"Where can I find them?"

The man bobbed his chin at the building. "At the meeting. Where else?" He blinked. "Wait a minute. Who the hell are you?"

Slayne smiled. "You can call me Solo with your dying breath if you want." He whipped the MP5 up and around and triggered a three-round burst into the Aryan's chest. A moment later his earpiece crackled.

"Solo. I saw that. I'm coming over."

"Hold your position, Ricco. No one has noticed. We're still good."

Slayne climbed down. Bending, he slid his hands under the dead man's shoulders and dragged him toward the trailer, intending to shove him underneath and out of sight.

"Solo! You have five unfriendlies coming up on the other side. They're almost on top of you."

Slayne peered under the trailer and saw boots and shoes. He had no time to hide the body. Unfurling, he turned just as the Aryans came around the end of the trailer. He triggered two bursts and the first two men fell. The others darted back. He backed up, too, toward the cab.

"This is Ricco. I'm on my way."

A head popped out. Slayne fired, but the man ducked from sight. He saw Montoya racing from the east end of the parking lot, and it hit him that he hadn't heard from the other member of their Triad in several minutes.

"Thor, do you copy?"

There was no answer.

"Thor, answer me."

Still no response.

Slayne swore, and almost didn't hear the patter of running feet coming around the front of the cab. He whirled and let the Aryan have a burst full in the face.

"Solo!" Ricco reported. "One of them has a walkie-talkie!"

Slayne could guess what the man was doing: alerting those inside the factory and requesting reinforcements. The situation threatened to go from bad to FUBAR.

"Hurry, Ricco."

"Almost there."

Just then double doors at the front of the factory burst open and out spilled a swarm of two-legged hornets.

Slayne's immediate thought was: This is bad.

Soren Anderson reached the west side of the parking lot. He stood at the fence for all of thirty seconds and then did what he wasn't supposed to do. He wedged Mjolnir under the power belt, jumped up, and caught hold of the bar at the top of the fence. Another moment, and he was up and over and crouched on the other side.

Hundreds of yards away was the truck. Slayne was almost to it.

Soren unlimbered Mjolnir and headed for the factory. He noticed a side door, but when he got there it was locked. Farther on was a window. Someone had cracked it open a few inches. Raising it all the way, he slipped over the sill and found himself in a small office. He moved to a door and listened. All he heard were voices from deeper in the factory.

Soren eased out the doorway. A dark hall led to a stairwell at one end and toward the voices at the other end. He chose the stairwell. At the landing he hesitated. Should he go up or down? His gut said to go down.

The basement consisted of another hallway with doors

on both sides. Soren went from one to the next, opening them and poking in his head. The first room contained boxes and crates. The next had shelves lined with medical supplies. The third was crammed with K rations.

Soren decided the building was some sort of supply depot. He opened the fourth door and nearly gagged. The reek was abominable. Urine and worse. It was pitch black. He saw nothing to show the room was in use and went to close the door.

Someone groaned.

Soren pushed the door all the way open. He held Mjolnir in front of him and switched it to its lowest power setting but didn't press the rune to fire. There was a hum and the weapon's head glowed just enough for him to see a pile of rags in the middle of the floor. As he looked, the pile of rags moved.

It was a black man. He had been terribly, brutally beaten. One eye was swollen shut, the other a slit. His nose was bent, his lips were pulped. His body was even worse. He was bound, wrists and ankles.

Soren sank to one knee and gently touched the man's shoulder. "Are you Ben Thomas?"

The slit of an eye twitched. The pulped lips moved. "Yes," he croaked.

"Odin has guided me to you so that I may save you."

"Odin?" A dry gourd rattled in the apparition's throat. "It's finally happened. I've gone nuts."

"The world is insane, friend Thomas, not you." Soren pried at the knots. "The human race has had its own Ragnarok. But we will rise anew, and the Ancient Way will be strong again." He had removed both ropes and was slipping his arm under Thomas to lift him when he heard footsteps in the hall. Turning Mjolnir off, he moved over against the wall near the door.

The footsteps drew closer.

"Whoa. What's this? Who's been in here?"

A figure entered, diminutive and female. A hand reached out and the room flooded with light from an overhead bulb. She held a tray with a bowl of soup, and took a step toward Thomas.

"Ben! How did you get free?"

Soren moved between her and the doorway so she couldn't get away. "Who are you?" he demanded.

The girl whirled. She gasped and her eyes grew wide with astonishment. "Damn. They grow them big where you come from."

"I will ask you again. Who are you?"

Recovering her composure, the girl snapped, "You've got that backwards, bozo. Who are *you* and what are you doing in here with my friend? If you're here to hurt him . . ."

"You are Mr. Thomas's friend?"

"That's what I said. Don't your ears work?"

"Then I will take both of you." Soren strode past her and again bent to lift Thomas.

"Hold on. Not so fast. Who the hell are you? And where do you think you're taking us?"

"I'm called Thor. I'm here with other Warriors to retrieve the vehicle Mr. Thomas was to deliver to our Home."

"Others?" Hope lit the girl's face. "God, I hope you brought a whole army."

"There are three of us."

Disappointment replaced the hope. "Only three? Damn, mister. Do you have any idea what you're up against? This is where the Aryan Army meets. There are pretty near sixty of their soldiers upstairs right this minute."

"Don't worry. I have Mjolnir."

"You have what?"

Soren held out the hammer. "Mjolnir. Crusher. Giant killer. Bringer of the lightning."

"God, you're nuts."

"I am perfectly sane, child. Who are you, by the way?"

"My friends call me Space. I suppose a lunatic can, too."

Soren turned with Thomas cradled under one arm. Instantly, Space set down the tray and was at their side. She slid her arm around Thomas from the other side.

Soren was surprised at how light the man was, and remarked as much.

"I sneak him food when I can but it's nowhere near enough. They keep a close eye on me." Space shifted so Ben's head rested on her shoulder. "They have me working in the kitchen. Me! Peeling spuds and chopping carrots. It's too damn stupid for words."

"At least they haven't killed either of you."

"They're keeping me around for breeding purposes. Their very words." Space tenderly touched Thomas's sunken cheek. "They've been trying to make Ben tell them how they can get into that vehicle of yours, but he wouldn't. That's the only reason he's still breathing."

"We'll get you to the Home, child. You'll be safe there."

"Whose home? Yours? Where is it?"

"I'll explain later. Right now we must hurry."

They carried Ben Thomas out of the room and down the hall to the stairs. His feet dragged until Soren noticed and raised him higher.

"We've got to take it slow, mister. If we run into any of the Aryans and they sound the alarm, you'll be up to your armpits in racists."

"Don't worry. I'll protect you."

Space angrily stamped a foot. "Damn it. You're not taking this serious enough. Didn't you hear me about the big meeting?"

"Didn't you hear me about Mjolnir?"

"Listen, nutjob. You have a hammer. They have guns. Lots and lots of guns. You won't stand a snowball's chance in hell. Our best bet is to sneak out before they notice I'm missing and come looking for me."

Soren was paying attention to her and not their surroundings. He realized his mistake when they came to the landing and he looked up to find five well-armed men staring at them in amazement.

"Hold it right there!" one of them barked, and leveled a rifle.

Brothers in Arms

Robert Montoya was within twenty yards of the trailer. He had angled across the lot to come up on it from the rear. The Aryans behind it hadn't seen him, and their backs were to him, which made no difference. Raising the Jati-Matic, he cut loose, felling them in their tracks.

Montoya started around the trailer to join Slayne. He had only taken a few steps when the front doors of the factory slammed open and out rushed more Aryans. Caught in the open, he had no choice but to dive flat and spray lead.

Slayne did the same. Their combined hailstorm drove the Aryans inside, leaving half a dozen on the ground. "Get up here, Ricco. I'll cover you."

Montoya didn't hesitate. He had a lot of open space to cover, but he had confidence in Slayne. He'd seen Slayne at target practice; the man seldom missed. He ran flat out.

Slayne saw a head appear in the doorway and let off a

burst to discourage any attempt to shoot Montoya. He watched the windows, too, and when a shadow filled one of them, he gave the shadow some slugs to chew on.

Montoya was almost to the cab when a single shot cracked. He felt the sting of impact and his left leg was nearly knocked out from under him. Limping, he returned fire and reached Slayne's side.

Slayne downed the shooter, an Aryan who had popped out of the open doorway. "Where are you hit?"

"The calf, I think. But I can manage." Montoya fired at a window. "What do we do? We can't stay here."

Slayne agreed. They were too exposed. They could take cover under the trailer, but the bottom was too high off the ground. Only the tires offered any protection, and he didn't want them shot out. He pointed at a pair of large metal trash bins at the near corner of the building. "There," he said. "You first. I've got your back."

Montoya nodded. His leg pained him with every step and he hopped more than he ran but he made good speed. The possibility of taking a round in the back lent extra incentive.

No shots rang out. Slayne kept expecting the Aryans to barrel from the factory in pursuit, but either they were regrouping or they had some other tactic up their sleeve. He reminded himself these weren't professionals. They were ordinary citizens with little if any combat training.

The Warriors were almost to the bins.

That was when men poured from the double doors, all of them firing at once.

Slayne and Montoya snapped off bursts but couldn't drive the Aryans back. Montoya reached a bin and crouched. Slayne darted behind the other one so they had a wider field of fire.

One Aryan was barking commands and the rest were

spreading out. The smart ones flattened and fired from prone positions.

Slayne did a scan and count. There had to be thirty or more. The odds were much too high. "Grenade."

Montoya quickly leaned the Jati-Matic against the bin and slipped off his backpack. He took out an M67, pulled the grenade away from the pin, and cocked his arm. "Frag out!" he yelled, and threw the grenade in a high loop.

Then he pressed against the bin.

Slayne did the same. He counted off four seconds in his head.

The M67 went off. It had a blast radius of forty-five feet but could hurl shrapnel out to two hundred or more. There were screams and curses, and in retaliation the Aryans poured a withering firestorm into the trash bins.

Slayne could hardly get off a burst for all the slugs pinging and whining past.

Montoya clipped a man running toward them and nearly had his own ear taken off. The growl of an engine caused him to glance toward the front gate and the street beyond. A pickup loaded with reinforcements was hurtling toward the factory. "Incoming hostiles!"

"I see them."

"God, I wish I had that battle suit you showed me back at the Home. I'd lick these bastards single-handed."

Slayne's mouth became a grim slit. Here they were, pinned down, one of them wounded, and they were about to be flanked. They needed to get out of there, but they wouldn't get fifty feet in the open parking lot. They needed help and they needed it now. He said out loud what he had been thinking for some time: "Where the hell is Thor?"

Soren was in motion before the words were out of the Aryan's mouth. He smashed Mjolnir into the man's face and was rewarded with a *crunch* and a spray of scarlet. Without breaking stride, Soren swung at a second enemy and caught him on the ear. The *crunch* this time was louder. A third Aryan tried to draw a revolver, but Soren pivoted and slammed Mjolnir against his skull. Now there were only two. Until now they had been too stupefied to move, but they started to bring up rifles just as Soren reached them. He shattered a knee, and when the Aryan screamed and doubled over, crushed a cranium.

The last man fumbled with the lever on his rifle. He looked up and bleated in stark terror, "No!"

Mjolnir was a streak in Soren's hands. He stood over the five bodies, surveying them for signs of life.

"Dear God." Space came over, holding Ben Thomas with both arms.

"Damn, you got moves, mister. That was slick."

"We must hurry. My friends are in trouble." Soren could hear the sounds of a firefight out in the parking lot. "Can you keep up?"

"Don't worry about me. I'll be right behind you." Space hefted Ben, who mumbled something she couldn't make out.

"What is the shortest way out the front?"

"Down this hall and take a left and then a right and you're there. But we'll run into the Aryans."

"I *want* to run into them."

Soren pressed the rune that activated Mjolnir. The hammer hummed to life and he felt the throb of its power. He set it to Arc, at two million volts. The gunfire grew louder. They met with no opposition, and when they rounded the last corner and he saw the open double doors, he broke into a run. "Stay back until I clear the way."

The parking lot was a kill zone. Some Aryans were down but many more were converging on a pair of trash bins.

Soren stepped into the open. He needed to be closer. The Aryans were focused on the bins to the exclusion of all else. He raised Mjolnir aloft and gave voice to his battle cry, roaring at the top of his lungs, "Odin!"

Some of them heard. Some of them spun.

Lighting arced in vivid bolts that crackled and writhed. The very air flared bright. Men screamed, and died. Hearts burst. Brains were fried. Blood boiled in veins.

Behind the trash bin, Robert Montoya felt his skin itch all over. "*Madre de Dios*! It's Thor!"

"About damn time." Slayne saw that not all the Aryans were down. He dropped two. Several others were fleeing. He ignored them and turned toward the front gate just as a pickup hurtled into the parking lot. There had to be a dozen men in the bed and three more in the front seat.

Soren pointed Mjolnir. He set the hammer to Bolt instead of Arc, at the same power level, two million volts. He didn't know what effect it would have, but he thought it would at least stop the pickup. He pressed the rune and fired.

A white-hot bolt a foot wide leaped from the hammer to the pickup's hood, and the entire vehicle was enveloped in a crackling corona. The pickup skewed and slowed as screams filled the air and the men in the front seat and the men in the bed went into spastic fits. Bodies sagged or slumped or fell over the side. The pickup coasted to a halt, smoke rising from under the hood and from the dead.

"Jesus," Montoya breathed.

Soren switched off Mjolnir. There was no one left to slay. He turned, and the girl was in the doorway, incredulity on her face.

"Who *are* you?"

"I've already told you. I'm called Thor."

Patrick Slayne lent a shoulder to Montoya. He was as impressed as they were by the spectacular display, but he was also simmering mad. "Where the hell have you been? We nearly bought the farm."

Soren indicated the girl and the man she was holding. "This is Space and Ben Thomas."

"Thomas?" Slayne could see what the man had been through but it didn't blunt his fury. "Let me get this straight. You disobeyed orders. You left your post. You violated every rule of a combat op and put your fellow Warriors at risk without any warning to them. All on the off chance this man *might* still be alive and you *might* be able to find him and *might* be able to effect a rescue?"

"Lighten up, grump," Space said.

"Excuse me?"

"I'm with Ben. The guy who wouldn't tell those buttwipes that Thor just smacked down how to get into your stupid van. Ben nearly died for you and still might if you don't get your head out of your ass and help him, and I mean right now."

Slayne did a double take. He couldn't recall the last time anyone had talked to him like that. "Little lady—" He started to give her a verbal blistering, and then he looked at Ben Thomas, really looked at him, and his anger evaporated.

"What? Don't stand there like a lump. Help him, damn it. He needs water. He needs food. He needs a doctor." Space swallowed and coughed, and said, "Damn. Don't die, Ben."

Montoya said, "You care for him, pretty one."

"He's my friend. My only friend. Wait. Did you just call me pretty?"

Slayne came to a decision. "Thor, help her get him to

the truck. Ricco, can you manage with that leg? Cover us while I revive him and then I'll tend to you."

It took half a canteen, but Ben Thomas came around and squinted at them through the eye that wasn't swollen shut. "Kurt Carpenter sent you, you say? I figured he gave up on me."

Quickly, Slayne explained the situation, ending with, "The important thing now is for us to get out of here before they reorganize or help arrives from other towns. Where are the keys to your truck?"

Ben explained that a spare key was stuck to the bottom of the brake pedal. "I used that new epoxy paste so it will pry right off."

A Klaxon was sounding somewhere in Smelterville when Slayne triumphantly held up the key. "Bingo. Everyone in. I'll drive."

"The hell you will. No one drives my rig but me." Ben straightened and stepped clear of Space. "Hand them over."

Space grabbed his arm. "What do you think you're doing? Look at you. You can hardly stand up. Let Grumpy do it."

"How much experience do you have?" Ben asked Slayne.

"With a truck this size? None. But it shouldn't be hard. I drove a few convoy trucks when I was in the service."

Ben wriggled his fingers. "Gimme." They boosted him in and he inserted the key. With a silent prayer he turned it. The engine coughed and belched smoke, then died. Ben tried again with the same result.

"Maybe the battery is dead," Space said.

The third time, Semper Fi rumbled and shook and Ben kissed the steering wheel. It hurt his lips, but he didn't care. "Pile in, people. Space, you crawl up in the bunk and leave the seat for us men."

There was a short delay while Slayne examined Montoya's wound. The slug had missed the bone and gone through. Slayne cleaned it with peroxide and applied a Quick Aid bandage.

They climbed in. Thor took up so much space that Slayne and Montoya had to sit sideways. Ben noticed their expressions, and for the first time in many a day, he laughed. Then he thrust his hand out at the big man with the big hammer.

"I understand I owe my life to you. Thanks."

"You are most welcome. But you should thank Mjolnir."

Ben quirked an eyebrow, and even that hurt. "All right, gents and lady. Let's get this show on the road.

Thor sat on the edge of the seat, his legs wide, and pressed Mjolnir's handle to the clamp in the center of the power belt.

"What are you doing?" Space asked.

"Recharging." Thor pressed a stud and the belt made a noise like a thousand bees. "I might have need of Mjolnir again before we are out of this."

No one tried to stop them on their way out of Smelterville. In four miles they came to Kellogg and were confronted by a hastily arranged barrier of cars and a tractor.

Ben Thomas never slowed. He told everyone to get down and Space to curl into a ball up in the bunk. Semper Fi was doing eighty when Ben wheeled onto the left shoulder and the tires churned gravel. Lead whanged off the hood and pinged the grille. The windshield was hit several times, but the shots were high. With the roar of some mammoth beast, Semper Fi swept around the barrier.

Next was Osburn, but they had no trouble. They made it past Wallace, too. Last was the barricade east of Wallace. Unlike the other barrier, this one stretched the width of the highway and then some.

Ben braked well out of rifle range. "I'm open to suggestions."

"Let us out," Slayne said. "We'll deal with them and when it's safe you bring your rig."

"There are an awful lot of them," Space said.

Thor checked a meter on the power belt. He turned the belt off and opened his door. "I'll handle this."

"What?" Slayne tried to grab him but Montoya was between them. "What do you think you're doing?"

"Making up for leaving you two alone back at the factory." Thor slammed the door. He made no attempt to seek cover but walked down the center of the highway toward the barricade.

Slayne was practically beside himself. "He's going to get himself killed!" He went to slide past Montoya but Montoya grabbed his arm.

"Wait. They're not shooting. They're as puzzled as we are."

It was true. The Aryans were pointing and talking but not firing. One of their number climbed up onto the bed of a pickup and cupped his hands to his mouth. "Halt or we'll cut you down!"

Thor smiled and raised Mjolnir over his head. "In Odin's name I greet you!"

Ben had his head out his window and heard every word. "That man is stone cold crazy."

Thor continued to advance, Mjolnir held high so the Aryans could see it.

The man on the car cupped his hands again. "What is that you're holding? A sledgehammer?"

"I am Thor and this is Mjolnir."

Some of the Aryans looked at one another and several laughed. The man on the car laughed, too, and then shouted, "Mister, we have you covered with machine guns and rifles and a bazooka. You just keep coming with that silly hammer of yours."

Still smiling, Thor did. When he was close enough, still smiling, he set the hammer to Arc. Still smiling, he set the power level to four million volts. Still smiling, he gripped Mjolnir with both hands and held the hammer overhead.

"In Odin's name, I greet you!" he repeated. "And in Thor's name I send you to the halls of Valhalla." He pressed the rune that would call down the lightning.

"God in heaven!" Ben Thomas blurted.

The bolts were too many to count. Some were as thick as a man's arm. Others were pencil thin. Leaping and arcing and crackling and sizzling, they sought out the living conductors they were programmed to seek.

In the cab, Space gasped and put a hand to her throat. She had seen what Thor did to the men in Smelterville. She had seen him stop the pickup. Neither fully prepared her for this. She saw men contort and shriek and burn. She saw smoke rise from their twisted bodies and blood gush from their mouths. And when it was over, as Thor went among them finishing off those still alive, she giggled and said, "That there is one sweet hunk of manhood."

Stepping-Stone

It was evening, but the only way to tell was by a clock since the sky was always gray. A brisk wind from the northwest rustled the trees in the Home.

Kurt Carpenter and Professor Diana Trevor were taking a stroll along the moat, Carpenter with his hands clasped behind his back.

"What did you make of Slayne's report?" Carpenter asked.

"They did well, your Warriors."

"*Our* Warriors, you mean. They protect the entire Family, not just me."

"Thor did outstanding. But he troubles me some, Kurt. He actually believes that Odin and his namesake are real."

"His religion is beside the point. That man is just what we need. He's devoted to the Family and the Home, a perfect role model for the others. Have you seen how they look up to him?"

"They look up to all the Warriors. They've even taken to calling them by their code names."

"We all might have new names soon."

"How's that again?"

"I'll tell you about it later. For now, the important thing is that Alpha Triad made it back with the SEAL."

"You sure put a lot of stock in that thing."

"It's our gift to the future." Carpenter stopped and gazed about the compound. "I want the Home to endure, Diana. I don't want all my effort to have been in vain. I'd give anything to have a time machine so I could travel fifty or a hundred years into the future and see if the Family and the Home are still here."

"We can only hope."

Kurt Carpenter may not have a time machine, but you can get a glimpse one hundred years into the future with a special preview of *Fox Run*.

For 100 years after a nuclear holocaust annihilated civilization, the Family has eked out a meager existence in the wilds of what used to be Minnesota. But something is going wrong in the Home. People aren't living as long as they used to. Mutations are becoming more common. To ensure their survival, there's only one thing the Family can do: venture outside the compound walls for help.

Three of their best Warriors are chosen for the task—Blade, Hickok, and Geronimo. Each is a weapons specialist renowned for his cunning and battle skills, each a proud defender of their fledgling society. But when a band of barbarians attacks the Home, the newly formed Alpha Triad may find their mission over before it even begins and no one left to save.

Coming July 2009

The blasted dog pack still had his scent.

Blade paused, angry, his gray eyes smoldering, his head cocked to one side as he listened intently. How long had they been after him now? Sweat soaked his thick curly hair and caked his green canvas pants and tattered fatigue shirt to his muscular body. At least a dozen were on his trail. Their eager baying filled the morning air. They were close, too close, and narrowing the gap rapidly.

Just what he needed.

Blade ran, balancing the deer carcass on his broad right shoulder, hefting his bow in his left hand. The quiver of arrows on his back and the Bowie knife on each hip bounced as he moved. He'd never make it to the Home with the extra weight, and after the three days of tracking it took him to bag the buck, three days with little sleep and even less food, he wasn't about to abandon the meat to the dogs.

No way.

Blade knew he was only two miles from the Home, two

miles from shelter and comfort, two miles from help. But the others had no idea when he would return, they didn't know which direction he would be coming from, and they wouldn't be this far from the Home under normal circumstances, anyway. In short, he couldn't rely on help from his friends.

He was up the creek without a paddle.

Blade smiled grimly. Who was he kidding? He was up the creek without a canoe.

The howling was louder, closer. The fleetest of the pack had the blood scent strong in their nostrils, and the aroma goaded them to more speed.

Blade ran over the crest of a small hill, then paused. A natural clearing was forty yards away, half the distance down the hill. It was his best bet. He would see them coming. Even better, they wouldn't be able to sneak up on him and nip his hamstrings when his back was turned.

The first dog must have spotted him because a tremendous yowl split the dawn.

Blade hurried, running for all he was worth. The buck slowed him down, though, impeding him, and he knew he was in trouble, knew he wouldn't quite reach the clearing even before he heard the patter of rushing pads on the hard ground and then the ominous, throaty growl from a canine pursuer. He tried to turn but he was too late.

The dog hit him squarely in the center of his back. The buck absorbed the brunt of the brutal impact but the force was still sufficient to drive Blade to his knees. He dropped the deer and the bow and twisted, his right Bowie drawn and ready, held waist-high, the blade extended.

He'd show these bloodsuckers how he'd gotten his name.

The lead dog was a big one, called a German shepherd in the days before the Big Blast. Huge, hungry, and deadly, it curled its lips back to display long, sharp teeth. It crouched, its legs tensed to spring.

The bow had landed to one side. The buck was lying on the ground between them.

"Come and get it!" Blade hissed.

The dog obliged; the German shepherd leaped, snarling.

Blade sidestepped. His right hand flashed. The Bowie sliced into the dog, opening its neck, crimson spurting over the grass.

The dog yelped and landed unsteadily, stunned by the pain and the sudden loss of blood.

Blade put his Bowie in its sheath and scooped up the bow. He drew an arrow from his quiver and fired in one smooth, practiced motion, the next dog dead on its feet before it realized what had happened, and Blade was spinning, another arrow ready, because the pack was on him now, and the third dog was caught in midair, the arrow thudding into its heavy brown chest and stopping the animal cold.

The pack didn't miss a beat.

Another dog, a mixed breed, came in low and fast and struck Blade in the legs as he was notching an arrow to the string.

Blade fell, flinging the bow aside, grabbing his Bowie knives, one in each hand, and he rose to his feet, slashing every which way, frantically cutting and slicing, berserk. He lost count of the number of dogs he laid open, fur and dust and blood flying, the barking and yowling and snapping reaching a crescendo.

A Doberman pinscher fearlessly plowed into him, slamming into his chest, bowling him over.

The pack howled with glee and closed in.

Blade managed to bury a Bowie in the Doberman. He had given it his best shot, small consolation for failing to get the meat back to the Family.

Teeth bit into his calf.

Another dog had his left wrist in a vise grip.

Blade lunged with his other Bowie, driving the knife into a dog's throat.

He was surrounded by raging canines. Slavering jaws snapped and gnashed. He cut, sliced, thrust.

One of the dogs was abruptly picked up and smashed to the earth, and an instant later a blast from a .30-06 carried to Blade's ears. Another dog, the one gripping his wrist, twisted and dropped away, flesh and blood erupting from its neck.

Hickok, Blade figured.

A war whoop was added to the din.

And Geronimo.

Blade grinned, relieved, as the .30-06 continued to boom.

Four more of the dogs were down and the ones still able to move took off, making for the nearest cover, a stand of brush and trees.

The rifleman was reluctant to let them go. Two more dogs were dead before the remnant of the pack reached haven.

Had to be Hickok, Blade knew. Hickok was the best shot, and Geronimo would be loath to waste ammo.

Blade slowly stood, taking stock of his wounds. He was bleeding from a number of bites but none were particularly severe except for his left wrist. The bone was exposed. He angrily kicked the dog responsible.

"I think the critter is dead," someone commented.

"He's obviously not a dog lover," said another.

Blade turned.

"You've always got to do everything the hard way, pard," Hickok said.

"He likes to do things the hard way," Geronimo remarked. "He thinks it builds character."

Blade grinned at his two best friends.

"We came out of the woods at the bottom of the hill," Hickok said, pointing, "just as the dogs closed in on you. Had to fire and run at the same time. Tricky. I was hoping I wouldn't waste a bullet by accidentally hitting you." He laughed.

"You mean you were aiming at the dogs?" Geronimo pretended to be surprised.

Blade shook his head at their antics, delighted they were there.

Hickok examined the shot dogs, ensuring none were still alive, his lean frame coiled. He held his rifle in both hands, casually sweeping the barrel from side to side. A leather belt was draped around his hips, a holster hanging from each side, his prized ivory-handled .357s gleaming in the sun, reflecting the meticulous care and attention they received from their owner. And well they should. With a rifle, Geronimo and a few other Warriors might come close to tying Hickok, but with a handgun Hickok was unequaled in marksmanship, almost uncanny in his speed and ability to hit any target without consciously appearing to aim his revolver. The .357s were his by virtue of his skill.

He was called Hickok because he had selected it on his sixteenth birthday, at his Naming. One of the old history books called *The Gunfighters* told of a man long ago who was a legend with pistols, a man called Hickok, a tall man with blond hair and a sweeping mustache. It was fitting that sixteen-year-old Nathan, already a qualified member of the Warrior class at that early age, should select as his namesake that of the deadliest gunfighter of all time, simply because he, Nathan, was the most proficient gunman in the Family's history.

The Warriors were well trained.

While Hickok checked the dogs, Geronimo kept alert,

scanning the tree line, prepared for any assault. In contrast to the blond, thin Hickok, Geronimo was stocky and had black hair. Where Hickok had blue eyes, Geronimo had brown. Where Hickok was tall, Geronimo was short. Where Hickok had long hair and a mustache like his hero, Geronimo wore his hair cut short and his face was clean shaven. What Geronimo lacked in ability with a handgun, he more than made up for in other areas. Geronimo was the Family's supreme tracker, a legacy of his Indian heritage. Geronimo was proud of the Indian in his blood, despite the fact that Plato had informed him his blood contained, at most, one-eighth Blackfoot inheritance. Geronimo was a superb hunter, he was immensely strong, and his eyesight was spectacular at great distances. He was also their best trapper, his trap line in the winter months often being their single largest supplier of fresh meat and new skins. Even in the worst of weather, Geronimo always returned with food.

Blade motioned at the slain dogs. "Don't think I'm not grateful for the rescue, but how in the world did you know where to find me? Luck?"

"Design, Plato would say," Geronimo replied.

"He means," Hickok interjected, "that Hazel told us where to find you. Specifically, which direction you were coming from. The timing was strictly ours. I'm just glad we didn't stop to relieve ourselves."

Hazel. Blade had experienced the results of her unique power several times in the past. Hazel's official title was Chief Family Empath. The Family was blessed, currently, with six individuals with psychic capabilities. Hazel was the oldest, the one with the most sensitive nature.

"Why was Hazel homing in on me?" Blade asked Hickok.

"Plato asked her to." Hickok had completed his check of the dogs; they were all dead.

"Why?"

"We don't know ourselves," Geronimo answered. "But whatever it is, it's urgent. Plato sent us to get you back as fast as we could."

"I wonder what's up?" Blade asked, more to himself than to the others.

"Instructions?" Hickok requested.

Blade paused, pondering. He was the head of Alpha Triad, and as such he was responsible for issuing orders and implementing strategy. The Warriors were divided into four Triads, each with a designated leader. It was Plato who had paired Blade with Hickok and Geronimo. As Plato put it, their teaming "compensated for individual deficiencies and maximized potential achievement."

Plato should know. He was the Family Leader, the wisest man in the Family.

Hickok and Geronimo were waiting.

"We'll take the buck back, even if it does slow us down a bit," Blade directed. "The Family needs the food." He rubbed his hurt wrist.

"You okay?" Geronimo asked.

"I'll make it back." Blade pressed his torn wrist against his side, hoping to stop the dripping blood. The wound was deep but the veins had been spared and his blood loss was minor. He bent and retrieved his Bowie from the dead Doberman and slid both knives into their sheaths.

"Think we can use any of the dogs?" Hickok prodded one of the bodies with a toe.

"Too mangy," Geronimo stated. "Look at their hides. Sores and blisters everywhere. The pelts wouldn't do us much good, and the meat would be too stringy and tough. Who knows what diseases they're carrying?"

"Point taken." Blade nodded in agreement. "Okay. We take the buck and make tracks. Plato wouldn't want us without very good reason. Hickok, you take point but keep in constant visual contact. Geronimo, bring the buck. I'll bring up the rear."

Hickok was already in motion. Geronimo hefted the buck onto his shoulder, waited until Hickok was ten yards ahead, then followed.

Blade fell into step behind them, speculating on the explanation for Plato's summons. He drifted back in time to his first meeting with the remarkable scholar and philosopher. Of course, nineteen years ago, Plato hadn't been so old, nor Leader of the Family. Plato had been selected to that post only four years earlier, after Blade's father had been killed by a mutate. Blade remembered his first impression of Plato was one of extreme kindness, conveyed in gentle blue eyes, a perpetually wrinkled brow, and the long hair and beard, now gray but previously brown.

"So this is your pride and joy?" Plato had said to Blade's father. "And he's only five? Big for his age. I see he has his dad's dark hair and abnormal gray eyes."

Plato had knelt and studied Blade's youthful, earnest face. "There is character here. He will be a tribute to both his parents." Plato had stood, toying with his beard, as was his habit when deep in concentration. "Have you noticed that since the nuclear war, our records indicate each generation contains a proportionally higher percentage of offspring with hair and eye pigmentation of an unusual coloration and combination?" This fact, apparently, had greatly impressed the sage, and Blade had wondered why. Nineteen years later he still didn't know.

Blade's reverie was shattered by a low, piercing whistle from up ahead. The danger signal. He dropped, flattening on the rough ground, ignoring a stabbing pain in his wrist, and glanced at Geronimo.

Geronimo was prone, too, the buck to one side. He was staring toward Hickok.

There was a small rise covered with bushes in front of them. Hickok was crouched behind a large shrub, watching something on the other side. He turned and motioned for them to join him, but he placed a finger over his lips in cautious warning.

Blade followed Geronimo, crawling on his elbows and knees, his left wrist starting to throb.

"Mutate," Hickok whispered, and pointed.

Every time Blade saw one, he had an instinctive urge to puke his guts out.

They were disgusting, repulsive, an aberration of nature, the consequence of man tampering with forces better left alone.

This one, once, must have been a black bear.

"Ugly sucker, isn't it?" Hickok said.

An understatement, Blade thought.

The mutate stood on the bank of a small stream, the water not more than a foot deep. There was a pool below the rise, about twenty feet in diameter. The mutate was concentrating on the pool, evidently after fish. The general shape and size of the creature was that of a bear, and the snout resembled that of a bear, but the rest of the beast was deformed and distorted, grotesque and bizarre. Its black hair was gone, replaced by huge, blistering sores, oozing pus from a dozen points, and cracked, dry, peeling brown skin. Two mounds of green mucus rose in place of ears. The mutate breathed in wheezing gasps, its mouth slack, its tongue distended. Its teeth were yellow and rotted.

The stench was overpowering, and Blade could feel his stomach start to toss. "We'll swing wide to the south and avoid it," he whispered to the other two, and began to back away.

Hickok was still watching the mutate, and he saw it suddenly rear upright and sniff the breeze. The breeze was blowing from the thing to them so it shouldn't be able to detect their scent. Then he remembered the buck, and the blood, and wondered if the smell had carried to the mutate without a strong wind.

The mutate was still sniffing and eyeing the rise suspiciously.

Hickok placed his hands on his Colt Pythons.

The mutate shuffled forward and entered the stream, still on its hind legs. The massive head swiveled from side to side as its beady eyes searched for the source of the scent.

A hand dropped on Hickok's right shoulder. "Think it has our scent?" Blade asked.

"I reckon," Hickok laconically responded.

"Let's move."

They carefully edged backward and rejoined Geronimo, who was patiently waiting with the buck over his shoulder.

"It knows we're here," Geronimo said, immediately assessing the situation.

"Think so."

They hurried, Blade leading, Gerinomo in the middle, Hickok in the rear.

They had been traveling to the southeast. With the mutate blocking their path they were forced to bear south, intending to strike an easterly course later on.

The Home was only a mile and a half distant.

That fact worried Blade. A mutate this close to the Home was a potential danger to the Family, a very real and extremely deadly menace. Thank the Spirit that the Founder had erected the walls! Without the encircling protection afforded by the twenty-foot high brick walls, the Family would have long since been overrun by the proliferation of wild beasts. The surge in wildlife was inevitable with the decline of man.

"Maybe we've lost it," Hickok suggested.

The underbrush behind them crackled and snapped, and loud snorts punctuated the mutate's determined advance.

"Damn," Blade fumed, enraged. He thoroughly detested mutates, in all their varieties and manifestations. An ordinary black bear would avoid contact with humans, fearing the two-legged horrors as if they were walking death. But mutates, in whatever form, deviated from the norm. Every mutate, whether it had once been a bear, a horse, or even a frog, inexplicably craved meat and stalked living flesh with an insatiable appetite. No one, not even Plato, knew what caused a mutate, which was why Plato was particularly desirous of locating, capturing, or killing a young mutate, a mutate not in adult stages of growth. No one had ever seen any but adult mutates. Plato had mentioned, many times, that he was of the opinion that mutates were the result of the widespread chemical warfare initiated during the nuclear conflict. If radiation alone was the cause, logic dictated that humans would be affected, and there was not a single report in the entire Family history of a solitary human mutate. Plato had emphasized over and over that discovering the cause of the mutates was a Family priority. Within the past decade the mutate population had increased dramatically—by geometric progression, according to Plato—a fact fraught with devastating implications.

Blade paused, considering his options. If they continued on their course, even if they reached the Home, the mutate would follow them to the walls, would know where the Family lived. It might linger in the area, waiting for someone, anyone, to venture outside. Or it might return from time to time, hoping to catch a human in the open. Blade couldn't allow that to happen.

Hickok and Geronimo had stopped and were watching him, waiting.

Blade surveyed their surroundings. They were in a small hollow with trees on every side. The Spirit had smiled on them.

"We make our stand here," Blade announced.

Hickok smiled.

Geronimo, knowing what was expected of him, dropped the buck in the middle of the hollow.

"Find your spots."

"You better take this," Hickok said, and tossed his rifle.

Blade caught it in his good hand.

"At this range," Hickok went on, "my pistols will be just as effective as the long gun. Besides, your bow would hardly scratch a mutate that big."

Blade nodded. If the mutate followed them into the hollow, and there was every reason to believe it would, then it would enter from the north as they had done. That left three points to fire from.

Geronimo was already climbing the west side, his sturdy legs pumping.

He reached the top and glanced back, his green shirt and pants, sewn together from the remains of an old tent, making excellent camouflage. He disappeared into the trees.

Hickok started up the east slope. "Aim for the head," he said over a shoulder.

Frequently, whenever Warriors socialized, the subject turned to killing, to the best technique for downing prey and foes alike. Some advocated a heart shot, a few shots to the neck, but Hickok was adamant in his defense of the head shot as the only viable shot to take, whether with a firearm, a bow, or a slingshot. "If you're aiming to kill," Hickok had said one night when the Warriors were gathered around a roaring fire, "then aim to kill. Any shot but a head shot is a waste of time, not to mention a danger to yourself and to those you're protecting. If you hit a man or an animal in the chest or neck, or anywhere else except the head, they can still shoot back or keep coming. It takes several seconds, sometimes, for the shock of being hit to register, and those seconds can be fatal for you. But when you hit them in the head, the impact stuns them immediately. Take out their brain, you snuff them instantly. No mess, no fuss."

Sometimes, Blade reflected, Hickok could be as cold as ice.

Hickok was perched on the rim, his buckskin-clad frame hunched over as he intently watched their back trail. He motioned for Blade to hurry, then vanished behind a boulder.

The mutate must be getting close.

Blade slung the bow over his shoulder, gripped the rifle in both hands, and ran up the south slope. Dense brush covered it right up to the trees. He swung behind a trunk, and crouched.

Not a moment too soon.

The mutate appeared. It stopped, scanning the terrain, uncertain. Its eyes rested on the buck.

Come and get it, gruesome! Blade was eager for the kill.

The creature ambled forward slowly, cautiously, not satisfied with the setup, raw animal instinct warning it that something was wrong.

But the thing couldn't resist the buck. Mutates, like those tiny terrors, shrews, could never get enough to eat. They even ate one another. That fact, Plato maintained, was the primary reason that mutates hadn't taken over the land.

Yet.

The beast grunted. Evidently deciding it was safe, after all, it lumbered toward the buck.

Blade debated the best course of action. He only had seconds to decide.

If he waited for the mutate to reach the buck, they'd have the clearest shots. But if the mutate touched the deer, came in contact with the meat in any way, it would be useless as food for the Family. The carcass would be irretrievably contaminated. Anything a mutate handled had to be destroyed or removed from all possible human contact. So the question was: could the Family afford the loss of this meat?

No.

The thing was five yards from the buck, head held low, sniffing and slavering.

Blade stood and raised the rifle to his shoulder, quickly sighting, aiming for the head as Hickok had advised.

A glint of sunlight on the barrel of the .30-06 alerted the mutate and it threw itself to the left, sensing a trap and making for cover. For its bulk and size, it was amazingly fast.

Blade was forced to hurry his shot. The rifle bucked and boomed and the slug ripped into the mutate's neck, blood and yellowish-green pus spurting every which way.

The mutate twisted, snarling, and Geronimo opened up from the west rim, his shot tearing a furrow in the top of the mutate's head.

The thing was furious! It wanted to attack, to rend and tear and crush, but searing pain racked every cell in its body and it elected to run, to seek cover, then circle and pounce when its quarry was off guard. The mutate whirled and charged up the east side, bellowing with rage and frustration.

That was when Hickok closed the trap. He calmly came into view, planted his feet, and placed his hands on his Colts.

The mutate was twenty yards below. It roared when it spotted him blocking its escape.

Hickok didn't draw his .357s.

The mutate charged, its mouth wide, those horrible teeth exposed.

Hickok remained immobile.

"Now!" Blade screamed, wondering why his friend was waiting, and knowing the answer, knowing that Hickok thrived on excitement, that Hickok reveled in danger and adventure. He dreaded that this time, Hickok had gone too far, that the gunman had overestimated his ability.

In another few bounds the mutate would be on him.

That was when Hickok drew . . .

Continued in *Endworld #1: The Fox Run*

HAGGAI CARMON

Author of *The Red Syndrome*

The master criminal and con man known as the Chameleon has eluded international law enforcement for twenty years. Dan Gordon was sure he finally had him, but he was left empty-handed. Now he won't rest until the Chameleon is stopped. The Chameleon is actually more than a mere criminal — he's an undercover sleeper agent. But Gordon is more than he seems, too. He's an experienced hunter, trained by the Mossad, working now for the CIA.

The trail leads Gordon to unforeseen locales and surprising alliances. His hunt for the slippery Chameleon will send him undercover to Iran, surrounded by danger and betrayal on all sides. What he learns could affect the world's balance of power . . . if he makes it out of Tehran alive.

THE CHAMELEON CONSPIRACY

A Dan Gordon Intelligence Thriller ®

ISBN 13: 978-0-8439-6191-1

A CEECEE GALLAGHER THRILLER

STACY DITTRICH

AUTHOR OF *THE DEVIL'S CLOSET*

According to legend, Mary Jane was hanged as a witch and still haunts her grave. But when a teenage girl is found brutally murdered there, Detective CeeCee Gallagher knows no ghost is responsible. It's up to her to hunt down the very real killer before he strikes again. Her investigation will take her across the country and land her deep in the middle of a secret so shocking the locals have kept it hidden for a hundred years. With her career—and her life—on the line, CeeCee will have to face her darkest fears if she wants to uncover the truth about...

MARY JANE'S GRAVE

ISBN 13: 978-0-8439-6160-7

RAYMOND BENSON

INTERNATIONALLY BESTSELLING AUTHOR OF
A HARD DAY'S DEATH

Musicians in progressive rock bands in Chicago are being murdered—one by one. The local police have no clues, but several of the musicians who fear they're next on the hit list claim that the killer is a ghost from the past—a woman who was reported missing and presumed dead for over thirty years!

The Rockin' Security team is called into action. Spike and his partner, Suzanne Prescott, travel to Chicago to investigate the case, only to find that no one wants to talk. As Spike digs deeper, he begins to unearth a lode of deadly secrets involving sex, psychedelic drugs, and, of course, rock 'n' roll. And it isn't long before the private detective becomes a pawn in a very dangerous game.

DARK SIDE OF THE MORGUE

ISBN 13: 978-0-8439-6198-0

THE COFFIN SHIP

The giant supertanker *Prometheus*, the largest ship on Earth, sits at anchor in the Persian Gulf. In her tanks are 250,000 tons of crude oil. Somewhere on board is a crew member determined that she never completes her voyage to Europe. Already, many of the ship's officers have been killed in a mysterious "accident."

The fate of *Prometheus* rests in the hands of Richard Mariner, the tanker's new captain. It is his responsibility to battle human treachery and the dangers of the open sea to bring *Prometheus* to safe harbor. From the Persian Gulf to the storm-tossed Atlantic, Mariner and his crew will struggle against the elements while trying to uncover the elusive—and cunning—enemy in their midst.

PETER TONKIN

ISBN 13: 978-0-8439-6221-5

RISK FACTOR

"A gripping psychological thriller."
— *Publishers Weekly*

When they found the nurse she was already dead. Sitting next to her body, covered in blood and holding a knife, was seventeen-year-old Garret, a patient in the psychiatric ward of the hospital. Dr. Molly Katz can't believe it. She's Garret's doctor and she never thought he was capable of anything like this. But now a second nurse has been butchered. Who's stalking the hospital corridors for prey? Could it be Garret after all? As Molly fights to save Garret from the law and his own mind, the eyes of the killer have turned toward her... and her children.

"Compelling...fast-paced."
—*School Library Journal*

Charles Atkins

ISBN 13: 978-0-8439-6085-3